night hunt

nightSHADE

3

carey decevito

This book is an original publication of Emberlust Press.

Copyright © 2020 by Carey Decevito.

Decevito, Carey

Night Hunt / Carey Decevito / paperback edition

ISBN-13: 978-0-993827-70-9

Cover photography by Eric David Battershell

Cover design by Clarisse Tan, CT Cover Creations

Cover model: Charlie Garforth

Edits provided by Karen Hrdlicka

Proofing provided by Joanne Thompson

For my two girls. Whenever you feel lost, I will forever help you find your way. I love you.
—Mommy

acknowledgments

First and foremost, where would I be without the unconditional support of my family. This one was a tough one to get through with all the hurdles we had to jump over. Thank you for understanding the times I've had to hole myself in some quiet corner to get things done, for cheering me on, and being as excited as I was when those final words were written.

Eric David Battershell—your impeccable talent and unwavering friendship never ceases to amaze me—thank you for helping out with yet another amazing cover.

Charlie Garforth—my Caden. Your friendship and support means the world to me. I'm so glad to call you friend.

Karen Hrdlicka—lady, words evade me for all that you do. Thank you for your amazing insight to get this one polished and ready for everyone to see. You're amazing!

Joanne Thompson—you're a friend first and foremost, but your support and recommendations have deemed you indispensable in my little book world. You are my proofreader extraordinaire, and a great source of entertainment and cheer when I need it most.

My dearest reviewers and ARC family—without you, I wouldn't be able to put this or any of my books out there. I will forever appreciate having you all in my corner.

Bloggers, readers & fellow authors—the book community is one that can sometimes be easy to get lost into. Thank you for your support, your continued readership, and most of all, providing me with the kick in the ass I've most definitely needed to finish this one. I try my best to support and share everything out there, and it definitely doesn't go unnoticed that you pay it forward. I'll forever be in your debt.

prologue

"DO YOU THINK MOM WILL..." Willow's voice faded as the hairs on the back of my neck began to stand on end.

It felt as though someone was watching us.

I eyed our surroundings. We were in a small clearing—my sister a mere ten yards away—surrounded by the dense forest while our parents were back at the campsite. They'd asked me to keep an eye out for bears.

Just as quick as the prickly sensation came, it left.

Nothing's there, Aspen, I tell myself.

I shrugged the unsteady feeling off and turned back to the patch of blueberries and the pint-sized basket I was trying to fill.

Only a few minutes of peace existed before the distinct sound of a branch cracking underfoot had my head snapping in the direction where the sound had come from.

My sister was nowhere in sight.

"Willow?" I called out.

From the general direction I'd heard the snapping tree limbs come from came a muffle, but it was well past the trees and thus had me taking a step forward.

1

Voice shaky, I begged for a response as I breeched the tree-line. "Willow?" That's when I came face-to-face with what I thought at first to be a bear on two legs.

"She's mine," he rasped in a voice that seemed far too unused.

What shocked me was the absence of fear that had come from my sister.

"Mom!" I screamed. "Daddy...help!" I tried, knowing the point was moot, we were too far away for my family to hear.

"He's my friend, Pen," Willow's eyes rolled, and then she giggled when the behemoth hitched her up onto his shoulders. "We're going to go play in the woods, now."

Bile rose from the pit of my stomach as panic set in. She was highly uneducated about stranger danger, having always gone everywhere with either myself or my parents.

"Put my sister down," I growled, then made to approach them as my sister's captor shook his head no and began backing away.

"Quiet," he grumbled.

I snorted my affront and put my fists to my hips as I kept stepping toward them. "If you don't put her down right now, you'll be in big trouble, mister!"

Before he could do or say anything, I went on the attack.

"You let her go!" I hollered, kicking at his shins as my sister giggled at his jostling.

All it took for the grizzly man was one simple push and I found myself on the flat of my back, my head making contact with solid rock.

My vision blurred, but my ears worked fine, beyond the subtle tinnitus.

"Come on, sweetheart," the thing rasped. "It's time to go."

"It's time for my surprise?" she squealed.

I tried to blink past the stars.

"Sure is, little bit."

Attempting to get back to my feet and fight for my sister's freedom, I toppled back to the forest floor, too woozy to do battle.

My mouth opened to scream, shriek...to simply say something, but nothing came out as I watched the stranger saunter away with my little sister waving goodbye over his shoulder, while I continued to fight for my voice.

A high-pitched wail had me sitting up with a start.

Taking in my surroundings, I realized I was surrounded by the four walls of my small cottage bedroom.

The cry that had awoken me only seconds earlier had come from none other than myself.

My mattress dipped as Molly, my five-year-old Australian shepherd made her approach, nuzzling my hand against the edge of the bed with a pitiful whine. Her sad eyes met mine and her tongue gave my digits a quick lick.

"I'm alright, girl," I whispered, my voice cracking from the abuse of my screams. "It was just another dream." I ruffled the fur atop her head while breathing to calm my racing heart.

It had been twenty-five years since then, but my dreams revived the horror of my youth far too vividly.

Willow's disappearance would always haunt me.

one

CADE

I'M GONNA KILL HIM, I thought as my phone rang with the *North Woods Law* theme song. Fucking Brycen and his technologically-inclined antics. All he had to do was replace the damn busted GPS chip in my phone and hand it back. I should have known the son of a bitch would play around.

"Yeah?" was my gruff answer.

"It's Rex."

"What's up?"

"Need your help with one of my skips."

Rex Dunham was a bounty hunter. When he wasn't busy chasing down criminals, he was helping Dalton Kippers and the rest of us part-timers—myself included—at Nightshade Securities Inc, or NSI.

"What do you have?" I asked.

Rex went on giving me the GPS coordinates to where he was, and I swallowed hard when he mentioned I'd most likely need my rappelling equipment since the idiot was halfway down a rock face, stuck in a crevasse.

"Hurry," the man urged.

I snorted. The guy was in a remote area. It was going to take me at least an hour to get to where he was, half of it lugging my pack and being on foot.

"The guy's not going anywhere, my friend."

"That's what you think. Fucker's so slimy I wouldn't put it past him to find a way out of there," he replied. "Just look for my tank," he referred to his large black Suburban.

"Out in five," I said, then hung up, shoving my phone back in my pocket. "Renegade!"

As his training dictated, my German shepherd came barreling toward me as I grabbed my radio off its charging base and jammed it in its rightful pocket of my backpack. The dog sat at my feet, hyperfocused and awaiting my next command.

"We've got work to do, bud." Cue the swishing tail, the only thing denoting his excitement. My boy loved to work.

As predicted, an hour and a few minutes later, I saw Rex's lone form standing with his back to me.

"About fucking time, asshole," he grumped.

"Pipe down, bitch. I'm here to save your ass, aren't I? Just be glad I'm not asking you for a cut of the profits." Lord knows he makes a killing with his own business, which always made me wonder why he'd even take up the extra gigs for NSI.

The man smirked, then grinned down when Renegade trotted up to him, nudging his hand.

"Hey, boy," he greeted, scratching my furry partner behind the ears. "He's about fifteen feet behind me, down about—I'd say—ten to twelve feet."

Nodding my head in understanding, I left Rex and Renegade to finish greeting one another while I approached the rather crumbly ledge of the cliff. Looking over, I spotted the guy.

"You alright down there?" I hollered.

"Fuck you!" was his answer.

Snorting my distaste for the man already, I set my backpack down and began pulling out my harness, some rope and carabiners. "You've got a gem there, Rex."

"You assholes done commiserating up there?" the idiot bellowed. "I'd like to get out of here before the vultures get to me."

"Pipe down, fuckhole!" Rex snarked, then turned to me. "Because that's exactly what he'll be when the boys in the pen find out what he's being locked up for."

I didn't want to know. I'd seen far too much bad shit in my thirty-seven years to need another mental picture to cloud over what little shroud of light I still had in my life.

As soon as I'd gone over the edge, I should have known something wasn't right. Renegade never whined when we worked—unless something was wrong.

That was my first hint.

The second came in the form of a thump up above and a muffled groan while I was prying Rex's skip's ankle free. Nothing but a fucking scratch, the bastard. He'd been lucky.

By the time I'd gotten to the top of the ledge, ignoring the raised hairs on the back of my neck, it wasn't long before I regretted my good Samaritan act.

Within seconds, Randall What's-his-face had been pulled up to safety, then I witnessed a large body fly over my head.

Next, I was the one plummeting downward...

The last thing I saw—or what I thought I saw—was a bear of a man.

No, that can't be right.

And the final thing I heard was Renegade howling off in the distance.

Then everything went black.

two

MY CUE TO get out of bed and get my day started came in the form of my fifty-five-pound, blue merle Aussie, Molly.

First, a wet nose to the cheek.

Then a lick.

A groan followed.

When I proceeded to ignore her, she did what got me going fastest...she crawled onto the bed from the foot, missing all crucial body parts that would inflict pain, then proceeded to lavish me with morning doggy-breath kisses that had me giggling in five seconds flat, not to mention, forgetting the remnants of my earlier rude awakening.

"Okay, okay!" I laughed as I pushed her off me, unable to smile at those sweet two-toned eyes of hers. "I get it. You're hungry, and you want to go see what you can hunt down for breakfast, even though we both know I give you far too much kibble already." She sat pretty at my side, sheets in a tangled mess, and looked at me as though I was missing something. I was. "And I guess you'd love nothing more than to relieve that stressed bladder of yours too, huh?"

A bark was my reply, along with wildly shaking hind quarters due to her docked tail.

As soon as my feet touched the floor, Molly was out the door, claws clicking toward the front entrance to my tiny home. When she decided I wasn't moving fast enough for her liking, a huff followed to signal her impatience as it always did.

"I'm coming, I'm coming." I rubbed at my eyes, reaching for the lock on the front door, then turned the knob and pulled inward. Molly was out of sight within two-point-five seconds flat, the only thing left behind was a trailing bark of happiness.

Having settled in with a freshly brewed cup of coffee and a ham and cheese omelette, I'd managed to polish off half of my breakfast before I heard my pooch's telltale thump on the front porch.

What had me curious, however, was the absence of pawing at my front door. Normally, by now, she'd want to eat, then get to her bed by the fireplace and curl up while I worked.

After five minutes passed, I grew even more curious, seeing as Molly had yet to signal her need to enter and devour her breakfast, as per her usual. I swear, I don't need an alarm clock to tell me what comes next in my day. Molly does that for me.

Leaving my last half of burnt toast to the side, I chewed the sawdust-like bite, swallowed it as I headed to see what was going on, grabbing my trusty Timber Classic Marlin 336C—which always sat inside a hidden nook in the cabinet by the front door—and made my way out to the porch wielding my weapon. A woman alone in a cottage in the woods could never be too careful.

"Who's there?" I shouted loud enough for someone in the remote vicinity of my sanctuary to hear me. "Show yourself!"

Molly came trotting from around the left side of the cottage, pausing to look behind her, then sat as if she was waiting on something...or someone. It wasn't like her. In fact, Molly didn't like strangers on her turf. She was highly protective of me and what we called our home. Hell, I'd had to shoot at a bear that came too close once because Molly thought she could take the damn thing on.

"Molly, come!"

The look of wanting to obey crossed her gaze as her eyes met mine, but she bowed her head and whined, then looked behind her again. Something told me whatever it was that had her attention wasn't a threat, so I sat the rifle down against the wooden railing to the porch and went to my dog.

"What is it, girl?"

A whimper. Not from my dog, however.

Huh?

As soon as I reached the front left side of my cottage, Molly trotted toward a massive German shepherd that sat there expectantly. She licked his snout, then nuzzled his neck, then came to my side and sat prettily.

"Hey there," I said calmly, then crouched down, noticing the dog had a collar on him, and some kind of harness to boot. Whoever's dog this was, the owner hadn't deserted him. "Come 'ere."

As soon as I'd said the words, the large ball of fur pounced on me, knocking me on my ass and killed me with whiny kisses. Molly hopped about, barking happily that her new friend and I were hitting it off.

"Off!" I commanded, albeit still gently, seeing that as friendly as this dog seemed to be, who knew how skittish he could be depending on what he'd been through.

The words were out, and the furry creature simply backed away, sat, and waited at attention.

Hmm.

"Stay," I said, as I regained my feet and decided to check out his collar.

Renegade.

I stood up and looked him over. A male. Unneutered. No obvious injuries. He looked clean and well-groomed; nails perfectly trimmed too.

With one bark, he ran toward the woods.

"No!" I shouted.

He dropped to a sit, then got back up, motioning with his head toward the tree line. With a sad whine, he began pacing, but wouldn't come back toward me. Then Molly trotted up to him and did what she always did best. She tried to console him in her own doggie way.

"Stay, guys," I said firmly.

No sooner had I admired the affection shared between the two canines, and called my order, they darted into the woods barking.

Shocked at Molly's defiance, my feet froze to the ground for a moment too long. As I set them in motion to follow, I realized I wasn't quite dressed for a trek in the woods; and who knew how far I'd be going.

Making a dash for the front door, I traded my slippers for my running shoes, grabbed a sweater to cover up my thinning, strappy nightgown and headed back out.

Molly had returned, barking to get my attention.

"Where is he, girl?" I cooed as she nuzzled my hand. Something wasn't right.

With one lick, she was off like a shot.

. . .

We had caught up to Renegade who had led us toward a rock face. To be honest, it hadn't been that far from my cottage— only half an hour or so of zig-zagging through the woods. The cliff was maybe twenty feet up above my head in some spots. It's a place I was familiar with, having come here to sit on the smooth bottom to work and sun myself in the bowels of nature when my cottage became a little too claustrophobic.

Some preferred a Starbucks, or even a library, but I would rather be one with Mother Nature. There was less judgment; fewer problems out here instead of dealing with civilization.

Bark.

As I looked toward where Renegade signaled from, I noticed a large lump of camouflage and black. It didn't take me long to move forward where Renegade laid himself next to what I now assumed was his owner.

Clearly out cold, the massive man lay there in a crumpled lump. Not too far from him, I noticed an even larger lump, if that were possible. This one was full of hair, wore a red plaid shirt, and his hidden face seemed crushed, neck positioned at an unnatural angle. It didn't take a genius to know the man-thing was no longer alive.

I shivered. That crumpled boulder of hair and limbs brought back far too many memories.

I have to get out of here.

Looking down, my hand reached of its own accord toward the seemingly sleeping man's throat.

Renegade growled.

"Easy, boy," I cooed. "I'm guessing this is your owner, huh? I'm just going to look him over, okay?"

He let out a whine which I took as permission.

Harness...frayed rope...carabiners. This guy must have been climbing the ledge up above.

And the dead body only fifteen feet over...

What the fuck happened here?

Using the training instilled in me since childhood—having physicians for parents sure came in handy—I palpated from his knees up, careful not to touch things that simply didn't need feeling.

Everything looked good with his hips.

Then I did his arms. No broken wrists, a few abrasions on his inner palms and a missing nail on his right middle finger, which I equated to him possibly having tried to claw for a good grip to stop his fall.

By the time I got to his head however, I knew why this man was out. The goose egg on the back of his skull had ruptured and I felt the wetness of blood. Not a lot, but enough to have my stomach start to roll.

There's a reason I never followed in my parents' footsteps. The sight of blood and I never really meshed well.

If I moved him, I'd have to find something to staunch the bleeding.

Move him, are you crazy? This guy must be at least two hundred pounds of solid muscle.

I huffed a breath, clearing the stray strand of hair out of my face before reaching for my nightgown and ripping part of the bottom to serve as a makeshift bandage.

After checking his neck and upper back, I wrapped the cloth around his head and over the lump, hoping it would hold for the length of our hike back. I found myself admiring the strong lines of his jaw, full lips, the light scruff of hair on his face, matching his dirty blond hair, and wondered what color his eyes were under those relaxed lids of his. He was striking in a rough, manly kind of way.

Woman, get your head out of the gutter.

Shaking myself back from my musings to the task at hand, I got up to my feet and looked toward my two canine companions.

"Guys, I'm going to need your help for this."

I swear Renegade gave me a nod in response.

three

IT TOOK me an hour and a half, and multiple breaks, to lug the dead weight of my mystery patient back to my cottage.

Another half an hour went by until I could get him up the porch, through my front door, and across the floor so I could heft him up and on to my bed.

Breathing heavily, I sighed while wiping the sweat off my forehead. Not once during my entire trek back had I heard or seen sign of life from him, and that had me worried.

Staring at the stranger in my bed, I began to doubt my capabilities. Perhaps I shouldn't have moved him, and then my mind went *there*...

This hadn't been the way I envisioned having a male in my space; and what a man he was.

Shaking the thought away, I proceeded with taking his boots off, setting them by the nightstand, and then moved to the kitchen to grab a bowl, filling it with warm soapy water.

After fetching my first aid kit and a cloth from my bathroom, I eased myself to sit next to him and started cleaning him up. I couldn't very well do much to help him on his healing journey until I knew exactly what I had to work with.

With my rather pitiful relationship with blood, I said a short prayer that I wouldn't have to stitch anything up.

Having to do so would surely throw me over the proverbial edge.

CADE

Motherfucker!

My head felt as though someone tried to run it over with a Mack truck.

Rex.

The cliff.

Fall.

Son of a bitch!

Running water.

Humming.

Sweet voice.

A dog whining.

I tried to open my eyes, but the mere speck of light had me clenching them closed as daggers stabbed at my brain.

Where the hell am I?

Forcing a single eye open, I briefly took in my surroundings, closing them once more. A cottage of sorts. Rustic yet quaint and definitely touched by a female hand. The smell of dog... soap...and was that lavender?

Whatever it was, it was soothing, and I found myself inhaling the relaxing fragrance.

Tilting my head to the side, I opened a single lid once more and a flash of skin whooshed by the doorway to my left.

Huh?

More humming, then an Amazon appeared before me in nothing but a white tank top, see-through where the droplets from her long, wet fiery hair had landed, and a pair of black hip-hugging shorts that showcased her long legs.

Mmm...Amazon...

No longer worried about my whereabouts, and pretty sure I was safe, I gave in to the darkness, letting it consume me once more.

Aspen

Throughout the day, I looked in on my patient who still had yet to wake.

To say I was worried would be an understatement.

Renegade refused to leave his owner's side for more than necessary, and thus Molly had lain at her new friend's side, holding vigil most of the time; the rest of the time, the duo spent either eating, drinking, or taking care of business.

With the house so quiet, I settled in my lounge chair with a cup of chamomile tea and a few oatmeal cookies I'd whipped up that afternoon and fired up my laptop. First, because I had no cell reception—things were spotty in my piece of the woods, and seemed to work whenever the wind blew just right—I had a message to send out to notify the authorities of the man I'd found and the cadaver in the woods, and then I'd get to the fun stuff. Work beckoned and my brain was filled with new ideas to write down after today's adventure. It was time for Penny to come out of her shell again.

"Make it stop," the hoarse voice startled me.

What? I looked up.

"Make the banging stop," the man lying in my bed grumbled anew as an arm flew up to ruffle his hair, causing him to wince. "Fuck."

I wanted to ask him if he was okay, or if he needed anything, but the flex in his bicep was so distracting, my tongue thickened and got itself stuck to the roof of my mouth.

Tsk. Tsk, Aspen. Maybe I should have focused on the action scenes instead of my characters getting it on if a simple contraction of a series of muscles had me practically melting into a puddle.

"Ren..."

Renegade released a whimper, then slowly climbed onto the bed to nuzzle his owner's face.

"He found me," I managed finally.

"Mmm." He basked in the love his pet offered him, then turned to face me, his eyes finally opening, but only slightly, and it was enough.

Blue.

No, that's not right. *Midnight* blue. Dark and beautiful, and I found my gaze fastened to his.

"Name."

"Huh?"

"Your name," he rasped. Something told me he sounded like this every day and not just when he woke.

"Pen...uh, Aspen," I stuttered.

"How'd I get here, Pen?"

A heated shiver coated my arms, making the hairs stand at attention. Oh, that deep rumble.

"I c—carried you," I answered. "I mean, Renegade found me, then brought you to me...or rather me to you, and there was this large bear...uh...a man who was dead not only twenty feet from you, and I bandaged you up with my favorite nightgown, and—" Deep breath. "And then I got the dogs to help me pull you back here. It wasn't easy. You're a big guy, and—"

A low rumble of laughter broke me from my bout of verbal diarrhea, causing me to bite my lip with jumpy nerves.

The man gave me a warm smile that did something to my lady parts.

Seriously, Aspen, get a hold of yourself! Haven't you heard of stranger danger?

"Thank you, Pen...or Aspen."

"You're welcome?" I squeaked out.

"I'm Cade."

"Is that short for something?"

"Albert," he divulged. "Albert Caden Summers. I prefer Caden or Cade. Have you seen my phone...or my radio? I need to call the guys and let them know I'm okay. And I need—"

"It was crushed," I interrupted. "It was by one of your hands when I found you. I tried to charge it because we have the same phones, but it wouldn't work...and there's no reception this far out, well, today anyway. I didn't see a radio, I'm sorry." I looked down toward my laptop and bit my lip again.

"What are you doing?"

Feeling as though I was caught in some sort of act I shouldn't have been performing, I quickly snapped the lid of my laptop shut and put the device on the side table, next to my empty mug of tea and a plateful of crumbs.

"Work." There was no way I was explaining to this stranger what I did to make ends meet. As successful as I was, I still wasn't comfortable divulging the details of my job to a mere stranger, especially a gorgeous one of the opposite sex.

"Work?" he eyed me suspiciously.

"Work," I repeated.

He smirked. "You're not going to give me more than that, are you?"

I simply shook my head from side to side.

Nope. Not happening.

CADE

She saved me.

Aspen had sheltered me, cleaned me up, and bandaged me.

I have my certification in first aid training, so I'm no slouch in giving medical assistance, but what the woman had done to me—*for* me—was beyond what I could have done for myself, or anyone else, out in the middle of nowhere in the state I had found myself in: concussed, sprained ankle but otherwise on the mend.

Who was this woman?

After our earlier exchange, she'd finally explained she was certain I had a concussion—I wouldn't argue with that, recognizing the nausea and marching band inside my head for what they were—a sprained ankle, a couple of bruises and a few scratches. When I'd looked at her questioningly about my bandaged finger, she'd practically gagged, telling me I'd lost a nail somehow. Trying to convey my gratitude had her looking uncomfortable. She'd run out of the bedroom, coming back with painkillers and a glass of water, which I took promptly because the percussion going on in my cranium was slowly driving me mad.

Next thing I knew, I'd faded into sleep.

I didn't want to come off as a creeper, but when I woke up next, I couldn't help but watch my savior as she typed away like a madwoman. Seriously, she could rival Brycen and Devolin—my coworkers at NSI and my boss's woman—for typing speed. She had to be a writer of some sort, or that was my guess.

Aspen was so enthralled in whatever it was she was working on she never saw how fixated I was on her. Every now and again, she'd take a moment to pause, play with her long mane of red hair, or sometimes chewing on her thumbnail, mumbling nonsensical words I couldn't make out from across the room, then went back to her typing.

I'd lost count of how many times I'd been in and out of consciousness, or how long I'd watched her when a "I know you're awake," broke me from my musings.

What gave me away?

"Your dog's tail starts its frantic wagging whenever you're conscious," she explained, a subtle smirk quirking the side of her lips, but her eyes never left her screen.

Fuck.

She giggled; the sweetest sound I'd heard come from her yet.

"Dinner?" She cleared her throat, then looked up from her computer. "Would you like something to eat?" She shut the top, then placed the laptop to the side, getting up. "I made enough for you in case you were hungry when you woke next. I'm sorry I've already eaten, but I can warm your bowl of stew up for you, if you'd like."

"You made stew?" I looked at her as if she'd lost her mind, then attempted to sit up.

Big mistake.

The room began to spin, I could feel the color draining from my face, and Aspen charged toward me, settling her hands on my shoulders, steadying me.

"Easy now," she said, reaching over me to grab a pillow,

"that knock to your head was a solid one. Let me help." She stood up, shifted the pillow to her right hand and from the side, offered her left for me to take.

"I can do it," I mumbled, trying to get the spinning to stop with deep breaths, seeing as closing my eyes made it worse.

"Just take my hand for some stability, will you?" she huffed.

I didn't bother nodding, thinking it would make things worse for me, and simply grabbed hold of her hand as she quite aptly pulled me forward, tossed the pillow behind my back, then eased me backward.

"Better?" she asked after I'd had a chance to settle back.

I stared at her. "It is. Thanks."

"I'll just go..." She threw her thumb in the direction of the door, then scampered off, leaving me baffled.

She worked a job where she can live in the remote woods where no one would dare doing so.

By herself.

She clearly knew her way around medical care.

And damn! Judging by the smell wafting my way...she surely knew how to cook.

But how does she find...

"It's been in the crockpot since before I baked the cookies earlier," she explained, making me jump at her stealthy reappearance.

My eyes widened. The woman knew her way to my heart, err...stomach, and had no idea. I had a sweet tooth of epic proportions and a voracious appetite for all things that came before dessert. "You bake too?"

She nodded, biting her lip, then proceeded to hand me the bowl of stew she held, then backed toward the bedroom door. "I forgot your water. Please eat. You can't get better if you don't get some sustenance in you."

She was right. What I hadn't expected, despite all the sleeping I'd already achieved, was I'd fall into a food coma shortly after I'd scarfed down the food, when I would have rather preferred to talk with Aspen and gotten to know her better.

I had to go—like something fierce—but I could barely sit up, let alone think about making my way to my feet.

"What's wrong?" Aspen asked, looking up from that laptop of hers. "You've been fidgeting for the last fifteen minutes. It's distracting me from my work."

I rolled my eyes. I couldn't believe I was about to ask for that kind of help.

"Cade?"

"Facilities," I mumbled, hating the words forming on my tongue. "I need the bathroom." I could feel the blush climbing my neck, heading toward my cheeks.

Within seconds, she was at my side, helping me to my one good leg like the no-nonsense woman I'd gleaned her to be. Like before, the room began to spin.

"Right. Up with you and slowly," she ordered, "then back to bed. You're not hurting yourself worse on my watch. Take it easy on that ankle, too. I'm sure it's quite tender."

As we stood, I realized the top of her head was just above my chin. "How tall are you?" I blurted.

"What's it matter?" she questioned, tongue sticking out as she used her strength to keep me stable, the look altogether laughable.

"I'm six three. I'd put you at five nine."

"Close. Five ten," she said, then squeezed my waist, supporting my weight even more. "Now, let's go before you soak my floor with...well, let's just go."

This had me chuckling, then her pinch to my side had me moving.

Spitfire.

I liked it a whole lot.

four

ASPEN

FUCKING CHAIR!

My back was stiff, I had a kink in my neck, and I had barely slept a wink last night.

Having a stranger in your house would do that to someone. It didn't matter he couldn't even sit up for extended periods of time without dizziness setting in. Then there was the fact I was certain Cade had a concussion, so I had set my alarm to wake me up every couple of hours so I could wake him, ask him a few questions then let him fade into sleep again.

I knew staying here rather than heading to the nearest emergency room would lead to more inquiries into my life; and it's not like I wasn't already doing what the hospital staff would have done. The more rest Cade got, the clearer his mind would be, and I was sure his questions would come. So far, I'd managed to evade and turn his inquisitiveness to my advantage, getting him to talk about himself instead, but at some point, I knew I'd have to give him something. The question would be what.

I'd learned he loved his dog, and he was the youngest of three, his siblings being evil big sisters (this he said lovingly, with a grin on his face). I knew he did a lot outside if the tanned creases at his eyes and the darkness of his skin was anything to go by. At some point, I began to wonder where the tan lines led. This train of thought had me quickly pretend to feign sleep, where eventually, within minutes, he would also, leaving me wide awake and a total creeper as I inspected the interloper on my everyday life before I had to wake him again for another assessment.

"I told you, I could have shuffled over and made room for you," he grumbled, sitting himself against the headboard with more ease than yesterday. He ran his hands over his face and through the increasing scruff.

"You wouldn't want to sleep with a cold floppy fish like me," I muttered, as I got up and rummaged around in my closet for a sweatshirt. The cottage had cooled down overnight and since Cade had started a slight fever, I'd opted to let the fire in the stove burn out so it was easier to keep his temperature low.

"Seriously, we could have shared," he said. "I'd have stayed on my side and you would be more rested than you look right now. Are you sure you even slept?" He eyed me suspiciously as though he was on to me and my acting antics to randomly pull a Sleeping Beauty.

"Maybe," I said with a shoulder shrug, then headed for the bathroom to brush my teeth. As soon as I was done, I gave Cade a cursory glance and made my way to the bedroom door. "I set an extra toothbrush for you on the bathroom counter. Help yourself. I'll go let the dogs out, start breakfast, and bring it in to you as soon as it's ready." He simply looked at me as if I'd grown an extra appendage. "What?" Okay, so maybe the lack of sleep and the ache in my bones were making me a little abrupt with him before I realized our latest conundrum. "Did you

27

need my help getting there?" I asked with a softer, empathetic tone.

His mouth opened, then snapped shut. He gave me a short shake of the head.

Right. Leaving the man with what little pride he must have felt he had right then, I gave him the benefit of the doubt, and left him to his own devices. Okay, so I felt awkward with this morning-after scenario and I really wanted to get out of the room.

Tell yourself what you want, woman, but those abs...

CADE

I may have taken my time, realizing I'd gone and made Aspen feel uncomfortable for the umpteenth time since my waking that morning. When I made my way out of the bathroom, glad my ankle was accepting most of my weight, despite it being sore still, I took one look at the bed and decided I didn't want to get back in it just yet. Instead, I explored; no matter what my caretaker might have to say about it. I wasn't stupid or as gullible as she might have decided about me. I'd caught on to her tactics to evade the questions I'd asked to gain information about her. What I didn't get was why she wouldn't share even some subtle basics. Her stonewalling only made me more curious, wanting to discover what made her tick.

As soon as I'd gotten to the living area, the massive library lining one of her living room walls beckoned me forward.

There were so many books.

A few of my own favorites, and then...

Penny Sexton.

I repeated the name in my mind, wondering why it seemed familiar. There was an entire collection from said author.

Picking one of the books, I slid it out of its spot, glanced at the title on the spine, then turned it to see the front cover.

Fanned Fires.

I peered over my shoulder where Aspen had yet to acknowledge my presence and found her typing away at her kitchen island.

Did the woman ever quit?

And then it hit me.

I'd seen that same cover and many others, similar in theme, before it...on Dalton's coffee table, and at Nightshade when both Emberlyn and Devolin—my coworkers' Shane's and Dalton's women—gushed over the latest release. They'd often left them in the reception area, littering the little table along with a few magazines.

Mommy porn, huh?

Before I knew it, the paperback was snatched from my hand and shoved back on its shelf, but not without me noticing the author's picture on its back cover.

"Don't touch!" she scolded me, a blush on her face.

"You?" I asked, turning to face the woman at my side, my lips quirking upward.

"Me, what?" She shifted on her feet, another uncomfortable tick.

"You write that kind of shit?"

Her face flushed with red, an attractive look when combined with her emerald eyes and that auburn hair of hers. "Excuse me, did you just call my work *shit?*" she ground out.

Oops.

I lifted my hands, palms out in a peacekeeping gesture. "I didn't mean it like that," I paused. "I swear. What I meant is that... Well, you don't look like... So that's what... What I'm—"

Hands on her hips, barefooted toes tapping on the hardwood floor, she laid into me. "I write books. Damn good books.

It's how I make a living," she stated. "It's not mommy porn, it's not porn at all. Yes, I like detail in my scenes, and I admit they are creative at times. I'm good at it, and I don't plan on—"

"Whoa! Whoa!" I waved my hands in the air to show her I really hadn't meant to set her off.

"And by the way—"

"I think it's pretty awesome," I stated, hoping I'd defuse her temper. "I've seen your books on store shelves. My friends' women love them. I just didn't think before I spoke." I moved to grab her left hand and put it in mine, her dark pink lips forming an 'O.'

"I'm a bestseller. Multiple times over," she defended without as much heat to her tone this time, and I was glad.

"And from what I've heard, rightly so," I said, then turned toward her library once more, daintily running my fingers over the spines of her works. "Which one was your favorite to write?"

"Um...what?"

"I want to know which one is your favorite so I can start by reading it first," I told her, and I meant it.

The woman's eyes widened with surprise, but I was pretty sure laughing at her expression right then wasn't the right response, so I simply offered her a kind smile.

ASPEN

Was this guy for real or had the hit he sustained to his head in that fall knocked the good sense out of him?

Sure, I've had men read and review my work. That's nothing new to me; but talk about a one-eighty. He went from calling my life's blood *shit*, then proceeded with flattery, and now he wanted to read *me*?

"Your favorite, Aspen. What's your favorite?" he asked again.

My mouth opened, then snapped shut as I focused on his back while he continued to peruse my titles.

"Ah!" He reached out, then turned around to present me with *Sheltered Rescue*. "I'm guessing this one's it, since you have three copies of it and only one of the others."

He got it in one.

Damn him.

My eyes left the book, meeting his.

The man knew he was dead on I gathered, what with the smirk on his smug-looking face.

"I'm right, aren't I?"

"So what?" Who cared if he had me pegged within twenty-four hours of being in each other's presence?

"Do you mind if I read it?" he asked, his eyes showing concern.

Somehow that made the small smidgeon of humiliation that still lingered, dissipate. I shook my head from side to side and cleared my throat. He really was being genuine. "No." *Yes.*

"Good." He smiled. "You really should be proud of this, you know." Hobbling toward the couch, he lowered himself slowly, then settled in, even as he made to pull down the throw blanket I had draped on the back of the sofa over his legs and feet.

"The bed's that way," I said, my hand pointing behind me in the general vicinity of where my bedroom was. "And I am proud. Can we... Uh! Can we just stop talking about my writing now? And what's more, you shouldn't be reading with a concussion."

He snorted, then stated, "I'm bored of the bed. I'd help you cook, but as you can see," he pointed to his head, then lifted his foot, "I'm kind of useless."

"You're mouth works just fine," I grumbled, as I turned and

stomped toward the kitchen to check on the breakfast skillet I had baking in the oven. It should be just about done. Maybe if I kept his mouth full with food, conversation would be history.

Then I can go work outside. Or better yet, maybe I can drive him back to town and be done with him once and for all.

I didn't dwell with the slight bereft feeling last idea had left me with.

five

CADE

THIS BOOK WAS GOOD. Great even. So great I'd read so much, my head's been pounding for the last hour and the letters have started to blur. And my opinion of her work wasn't because I now knew the author, or the fact the hero in it worked in Search and Rescue, just like me. Her prose and syntax were right on the money, and I got a kick out of the edgy and sarcastic, sometimes comedic byplay between the characters—they were very much like her.

Then again, my praise would probably hold no weight, seeing as the woman in question had yet to come in for lunch after our earlier squabble.

After we'd eaten breakfast—albeit in uncomfortable silence —Aspen had disappeared to her room, then emerged a few minutes later with a pair of leggings and a loose T-shirt that fell off her shoulder, claiming she was heading outside to exercise the dogs and do a bit of yard work.

Throughout the morning, I heard barking, then silence. Eventually there was the telltale sound of an axe meeting wood.

The clucking is what got me out of my seat and heading to one of her small windows to see what the hell was going on.

Surrounded by nothing but forest, and a small, pebbled drive of sorts, I caught sight of Aspen heading toward the side of her home, her hair in total disarray and a light sheen of sweat over her brow. The woman grew more appealing in that instant —unafraid of hard, honest work—it was sexy.

Knowingly aware of her avoidance, I decided to take matters into my own hands.

Thank God the cottage wasn't a large one. I managed to jar my brain some by limping to the kitchen, in search of something to put together to eat. My head was killing me, but I needed food in me before I could take another painkiller. I'd noticed Aspen had left me some on her night table. Maybe I'd have a nap again, but that damn book was hard to put down, hence why I was giving my eyes and head a break—somewhat.

A search through her fridge brought a bowl of eggs, dated for what I guess were the days they'd been gathered. It explained the clucking outside too. Bread, mayo, mustard, fresh-cut lettuce, some leftover roasted chicken were located next. I had the makings of a couple of hefty sandwiches.

It took me a while to get settled on one of her barstools and make two sandwiches; and it took me even longer to hobble to the front door without throwing the food all over the place. The toothpicks on the side counter helped keep everything together, thankfully; and so did the plastic cling wrap over each plate.

Setting Aspen's lunch and the bottle of water I'd tucked under my arm on the small table that matched her two Adirondack chairs, I managed to hobble toward the side of the porch where I'd last seen the rather enigmatic woman disappear earlier.

"Lunch is ready!" I called.

Out from behind what I discovered was a small chicken coop, popped Aspen's head.

Her brows scrunched up in apparent confusion. "Did you say lunch?"

I nodded, then shrugged. "I figured I owed you one. Now clean up and come eat before the birds get it."

With that, I turned and hopped my way back inside to enjoy my meal on the couch with a good book. If I wasn't mistaken, I was about to see a bit inside Ms. Sexton's kinky mind in the next few chapters, and I couldn't wait.

ASPEN

He'd made me lunch.

He was hurt and now healing, and while I should have been the good nursemaid, he was the one taking care of me because I'd been such a wuss at confrontation.

I really should go apologize to him and explain why I am the way I am. After all, he hadn't meant to come off like a judgmental jerk before. He'd said so himself, and then he'd tried to boost my confidence about my writing which he'd earlier called *shit*.

So that was it. I was going to go eat my lunch—and then talk to Cade.

"Holy shit!" was blurted as soon as I stepped foot inside the door, followed by Cade dropping one of my couch's throw pillows over his crotch, the book—*my* book—he was reading, thrown haphazardly on the couch next to him.

"Good *shit*, huh?" I sassed, then walked by him, smirking as I gave him a moment to collect himself, and headed to put my plate in the kitchen sink to wash later with the breakfast dishes

I hadn't tackled. Lo and behold I had a surprise there too. Turning, I faced my visitor. "You washed the dishes?"

Not turning around to face me over the back of the couch, he nodded slightly, massaging at his temples. I knew his head was hurting, but he wasn't showing any sign of sleeping things off.

"You should be resting," I chided lightly, appreciative of his efforts, and a little amused that this larger-than-life man had a real interest in my work.

"Least I could do," he mumbled.

"Thanks." I bit my lip. "And thanks for the sandwich and water."

Another nod.

"Listen," I said, as I came back around the couch, then sat on the chair off to its side. It was my writing chair whenever it was a chilly night and I wanted to curl up and stay warm by the fire.

"I need to get out of your space, yeah, I know." He looked at me with sincerity strewn across his face. "I need to get to my truck, but with my head the way it is, I can't drive just yet. I didn't think of this before, but can I borrow your phone?"

I shook my head, no.

His eyes narrowed on me. "You're kidding, right?"

I shook my head again. "No, I'm not. Our cells aren't within range here on most days."

"What do you do in case of emergency?"

"I handle it myself."

"And what if you can't?"

I squared my shoulders and looked him straight in the eye. "I guess this poor wilting flower is just doomed to die out here all by her lonesome." When he didn't say anything further, I decided to humor him. "If I need anything, I have a sporadic internet connection that gets me what I want. If I'm in dire need of something, I have my Jeep to get me to the nearest town. I can rotate my tires, change my own oil, cut some lumber, and whatever else you might think women shouldn't know anything about. Contrary to what this place looks like, and what you might have assumed by looking around, I do make it out to civilization, Albert Caden Summers."

He chuckled. "You remind me of your heroine, Sasha." He grabbed the book he'd chucked to the side and waved it, then sighed. "So what's next?"

My brows knitted together in thought.

What was next?

My head reeled with confusing thoughts and emotions.

Shit if I knew!

CADE

I knew I should care more about what was going on with Rex, his skip, and the rest of the gang at Nightshade. Hell, I should be concerned about the dead dude who had been pushed off the cliff before I'd gone plummeting down it myself. With that said, there was no doubt in my mind Rex had gotten word back to the men about what had happened, or his rendition rather. And I knew Aspen had put in a message with the authorities about what she'd come across, or so she'd mentioned as much last night.

But I didn't care enough to force the situation and get out of her hair at the moment. I probably could have made my way back to town, but the dizzy spells that came and went over the course of the afternoon told me it had been a good call for me to stay put.

By dinnertime, my appetite was lost, my head was back to

pounding to the point I could barely keep my eyes open, and I was freezing.

"You need to eat," she said, as she saw me picking at my plate, only shuffling each ridiculously tasty-looking morsel around.

"I'm not..." I took a deep breath at the sudden wave of nausea that settled in my gut.

"Son of a biscuit!" I heard, then before I knew it, Aspen was at my side, preventing me from toppling off the side of the chair, then helping me up to my feet. "We need to get you into bed."

"Couch," I mumbled, not sure how much longer it would be before the contents of my stomach would come back to greet us, or if I'd end up passed out on the floor first.

"No," she argued. "The bed's closer, and you don't need another knock to the head to make things worse."

She won.

Teeth chattering, throbbing in my brain, my nausea finally settled with my lying facing the wall. The medicine did nothing this time around for my head or the fever I suspected I fell prey to. I had three large blankets over me, and I was still shaking.

"Cade," a gentle voice broke me away from all thoughts of my misery. "You need to strip, Caden."

"Not the time, sweetheart," I croaked, my throat having gone raw and dry.

A muffled laugh.

"I'm glad my pain is amusing," I mumbled, pulling the blankets over my head.

"No, Cade," she started, "I need you to take your clothes off so I can wash and dry them. You've soaked through them with your sweating."

"I'm not sweating," I argued. "I'm fucking freezing."

"Albert Caden Summers," she growled in that don't-mess-with-me kind of way women often excelled at—my mother especially.

"Fine," I grumbled, then sat myself up.

"Do you think you can get out of bed?" she asked. "I'll change the sheets while I'm at it."

Not giving her any more acknowledgement, I practically dragged myself to the bathroom, my arms wrapped around myself to calm the shaking whenever I wasn't holding on for dear life for fear of falling on my face, thanks to my body's weakness and spinning head.

"Feel better?" Aspen asked, as soon as I'd stepped foot into the bedroom a half hour or so later.

"Much," I said. I wasn't going to let her know I'd spent the latter part of the last fifteen minutes sitting on the bottom of her tub, in case I lost my balance.

When I'd entered the bathroom earlier, the shower was begging my attention, so I'd indulged, not even caring to ask for permission. It gave Aspen enough time to do her thing anyway. By the time I got out, my clothes were missing and all that was left was a sheet for me to cover up with on the bathroom counter. It never occurred to me that she could have gotten an eyeful considering her shower curtains were clear.

"I left some medicine and water for you on the bedside table," she said from her chair, her eyes aimed at that laptop of hers.

The sudden realization I was feeling parched hit me, so I made my way to the bed, sitting on the edge of the mattress, and grabbed the glass. I managed a, "Thank you," after I'd finished gulping down the drink.

Settling back down in the freshly made bed, I scooted sideways so as to make enough room for Aspen, then patted the mattress at my side. She couldn't even meet my eyes, the flush on her cheeks one of embarrassment, or was it shyness? "I could go and sleep on the couch," I offered. "I do feel better now." I was, but not by much. Truthfully, she looked absolutely exhausted, and I felt awful she'd barely slept a wink last night because she'd taken care of me.

"No," she croaked, then cleared her throat. "No, that's okay. You keep the bed and I'll take the couch."

"Aspen," I warned.

Our respective dogs watched the interchange from the carpet at the foot of the bed, snuggled closely together. I actually found myself envious of Renegade for once. The lucky bastard had someone to snuggle with and for once I'd found myself wanting what he had. Yes, that's me, jealous of a damn dog.

"Oh, fine!" she huffed, then got up from her nemesis chair from the night before and stomped toward the bed. That's when I noticed she'd changed.

But why cover the top with that ratty sweatshirt?

"I promise I'll keep the sheet wrapped around me. It seems a nymph made away with my clothes while I was showering." I smirked.

She scooted to the edge of the bed, grabbed the decorative pillows that were on the floor beside it, then shoved them between us, pummelling them each into the mattress to ensure they'd stay put throughout the night.

"Turn around," she demanded. "This is not what I thought sharing a bed with a man for the first time in this place would be like."

"I'm the one who's naked," I stated, *and I'm not touching that last comment.*

40

"Just turn around, will you?"

"Spoilsport," I mumbled, doing as she'd requested, then burying my face into the pillow because it had that lavender smell I'd sniffed yesterday in my delirious state.

"Be careful with that sarcasm or you might find yourself sleeping with the chickens," she muttered.

Within minutes, the room grew quiet and I couldn't help thinking about what was going through Aspen's head at that very moment.

Flipping myself around with my sore muscles groaning in protest, I turned to face her, finding her mummied in her blankets, her arms stiff on either side of her.

"Relax, sweetheart," I whispered, staying on my side of our fluffy divider.

"I'm trying." She let out a loud breath, and I swear I could see her slowly melting into the mattress.

"That's it," I cooed, then yawned. How could I be sleepy at a time like this? Oh yeah, I'm gimped out and that fever I'd spiked took just about all I had out of me.

"Tell me something more about you," she said. "I know about your family, but what do you do?"

So it was going to be more about me, huh? All right. Fine. If it made her feel more at ease, then why not. Maybe we'd get to talk more about why she thought she was frigid and why the fuck I was the first man in her bed later.

six

OH FUCK! *He's Search and Rescue?* The moment he told me, my body turned cold.

His little tidbit of information hit far too close to home in that instant.

"What?" he asked, propping himself up on his elbow and watching as I processed what he had divulged.

I shook my head, trying to rid the sting of tears that plagued my eyes. "Nothing," I mumbled.

"No, I know something's wrong," he said quietly. "What do you have against us? For crying out loud, I'm reading one of your books and the hero is someone who's in my line of work, so why would you—"

"Just drop it, Cade," I whispered, the fight over the stinging in my eyes was a losing one.

"Pen," he rasped, then reached his other hand to grasp mine.

"I've dealt with people in your business before," I gulped the lump in my throat. "My...my sister disappeared when I was twelve. We searched these woods for as long as we could. Search and Rescue, the local authorities, friends, family members, volunteers from our town and the area..."

It had been useless.

It had been my social life's demise too.

No one believed me.

"Believed what?" He pushed at the words I thought had only been in my head.

I shivered at the onslaught of memories. "I...I—"

"Take your time." He squeezed my hand.

"Someone took her." I looked at him to find that his eyes had widened at my unexpected information. "I fought him, and I screamed. No one came."

"Bear man," he whispered.

My eyes widened. "What?" Then I pushed his hand away as if it had burned me, and shot up to sit in bed. "W—what did you just say?"

"The legend of the bear man," he explained. I gulped as he sat up to mimic my position on the mattress. "When I was a kid, my father—who did the same thing I do now—came home talking about one of his cases. It's not because he didn't believe the kid who'd told him everything at the scene. Some didn't, and he'd come home talking nonsense and was pissed at the world for not going with his gut, which had always served him well."

I didn't get a good feeling about this, but like the masochist I seemed to be, I had to ask. "What happened?"

"He pushed until he was given the boot, then drank himself into liver failure and died a few years ago," he explained.

My heart went to him and his family for their share of hardships. I hadn't been alone in my suffering, as I always believed, and what Cade had just divulged proved it.

"Summers..." trailed off my tongue as I figured out why the

surname had sounded familiar when Cade had introduced himself yesterday, but nothing had immediately clicked. "Albert Summers."

"That's right," he said, smiling sadly. "My namesake. I'm surprised you remember."

How could I have forgotten the gentleness with which that man had treated me? He had been the only one who hadn't ridiculed me when he thought I wasn't around or listening.

"He was nice to me," I went on. "The only one who seemed to actually believe what I told him."

"It was the only case he never saw closed."

CADE

My mind was officially blown.

The girl who'd disappeared from school so long ago had returned. I remembered how much those in the hallways, between classes, had ridiculed her story, but I'd never gone along with their shenanigans. Maybe it was because I knew about her story from Dad, maybe it was because I knew what it felt like to be teased and bullied, because I'd gotten it too what with Dad being involved with the case.

So, I knew better back then.

And I knew better now.

"Sir Carter Junior High," I stated, getting a doubletake from the woman who sat beside me. "That's where you went to school."

"Only the best for the kid from physicians," she snarked.

I nodded. My parents had been lucky to get me in there through a scholarship. "I remember the day you never came back."

"I chose to follow Mom and Dad after junior high and do my

high school from home, if you can call a tent in the middle of Africa a home," she explained. "I'm glad I made that decision. It gave me a few more years with them."

I smiled at that. "I'm sure anywhere was better than at Carter," I stated. "Where are they now?"

"I lost them my senior year of college. I came back to the U.S. to do that," she explained. "They were on their way back from the Congo when their charter had a mechanical failure... something with the engine. They went down."

Dead.

Fuck.

"So, it's just me now; and my cottage...my dog."

"And your books," I added.

Her laugh came out dry, but her words sounded humored. "And my books," she nodded. As she settled herself back on the mattress, assuming the blanket mummy position like before, I smiled to myself, and shook my head, following suit. "You mentioned you had two jobs before all of this melodrama of mine."

"Hmm," I managed, as I propped my head up to watch her. She seemed to have warmed toward me once again.

Our eyes caught and held.

"And?" she smirked. "Are you going to tell me or is this some top-secret assignment thing where you'd have to off me if you told me?"

Chuckling, I looked down to the blankets, noticing the pillows weren't doing much of the work they were supposed to be doing anymore.

"I work part time for a private security firm," I explained. "Some security, mostly stuff where they can use my Search & Rescue skills to their advantage. That's the job I was doing when I fell."

Her excitement was palpable as she shifted. Forgetting

about her reservations, she mimicked my posture: on her side with her head propped up by one arm.

She grinned. "Do tell me more," she urged.

Knowing that the change in subject by talking about the gang at Nightshade would be of help to wipe the darkness of the earlier part of our conversation, I humored her with only the best stories, gaining myself full belly laughs instead of the few giggles I'd already received. Those sounds were the best and I found myself addicted to getting more out of her.

Before I knew it, I was wide awake, smiling, and admiring a slumbering Aspen, who snored softly, the subtle dribble of saliva gathering at the corner of her mouth, but never trickling over.

Christ, but she was cute.

seven

HEAT.

So much heat suffused my body as I woke up.

All was quiet in the house except for the clicking of claws on the floor.

I was comfortable, and didn't want to move from my little bubble, except my bladder chose that very moment to make its demands known, and it—not to mention a wet-nosed dog—forced me into action.

It wasn't until I started to get up that I realized why I was so warm. A large and heavy arm lay across my waist, holding me back against a hard surface.

Cade.

"Hmm?" he grumbled, then buried his nose into the hair at the back of my head.

Oh...that's real...nice. I smiled at this larger-than-life teddy bear, biting my lip so as not to let the moan of enjoyment escape me, then whispered, "Let go," even if it was the last thing I wanted.

"Don't wanna," he mumbled, sighing. Apparently, his sense of enjoyment matched mine.

"The dogs want out," I argued, albeit not very forcibly.

"They can wait," he said. He was right. "I barely slept a wink last night. You were right, sweetheart; you flop around like a fish."

I could feel the blood rush to my face, and my body froze at his words, the peace of the morning vanishing in their wake.

"But you're definitely not fucking cold," he finished with another nuzzle to emphasize his point, and I forced my body to relax.

Oh God!

"Cade, I really do have to get up," I gently tried to pry off his grip.

This wasn't happening. On a loud groan, then a squeeze that made my bladder scream, he released me.

Grabbing some clothes on the way to the bathroom, I threw the man a cursory glance and said, "I'll check on the laundry after I'm done and get you your clothes back."

Looking at him had been a huge mistake.

The man was a tatted-out God of the Woods of some sort, with only my side of the blankets covering his jewels and some of his legs.

Damn!

I slammed the bathroom door, leaned against it, closed my eyes, and took a series of deep breaths.

The man certainly didn't just look good...he gave good cuddle too.

And my mind wandered off, conjuring all sorts of scenarios he'd been inspiring since I'd rescued him in the forest of my past.

CADE

As soon as the door slammed behind her, I rolled to my back, not believing what had just happened.

I might as well have mauled her with the way she skittered away from me. First, a morning wood. Nothing new there and completely natural—and I hoped she understood that—but I had to cuddle up to her as if she was my most-prized possession, and what's more, I'd refused her freedom at first because spooning her felt so damn natural.

"You idiot," I cursed under my breath. There'd been a reason for those pillows after all. She didn't want anything to do with a strange man in her house, let alone in her bed. That much had been evident since she'd taken me in. She clearly wasn't keen on having anyone around, considering where she chose to live. Hell, I couldn't blame her for resisting and wanting to sleep on the couch, or even that godforsaken lounge chair that I could only describe as dating back to the late seventies. That thing deserved to be shredded and its guts used as firewood. Hell, whenever I got out of here, maybe I'd buy her a new one as a thank-you.

"Here." I felt the clothes being deposited at the foot of the bed by my feet, knocking me from my thoughts. "The dogs are outside. I'll get started on breakfast." Then she gestured wildly, motioning toward my naked torso. "You should cover up."

I didn't miss the lingering look of appreciation, combined with the profuse blush heating her cheeks, before she left the room though.

Aggressive barking followed by some shouting from Aspen and the slamming of a front door had me running—believe me, this wasn't easy, especially with subtle hints of my concussion remaining—to see what kind of hell had broken loose.

"Leave or I'll shoot!" my rescuer shouted.

"Ma'am, we're not here to hurt you," a voice I recognized said. "We just need you to take a look at this picture and tell us if you've seen this man."

"Don't come closer!" Then I heard Renegade's growl.

Oh shit!

"Ren, off!" That was Dalton's voice.

More growling.

"Shit, D, he's not listening." That was Rex. "What the fuck?"

"I don't know, man," he said. "Maybe it's not him."

"He's wearing the same getup Cade puts on him when he's working. Of course, it's him!" Rex said. "He was sporting it two days ago."

"Ma'am, if you could get Cujo there to back off, I'd be grateful," Dalton requested in that cool and controlled manner of his. "My name is Dalton Kippers. I own Nightshade Securities in the next town over. I see you have our friend's dog here. If Renegade is around, there's reason for us to believe that you might have seen his owner. His name is Albert Caden Summers."

Renegade growled and a higher pitched whine—one I figured belonging to Molly—joined him.

I'd barely made it out the door in time to find Aspen pointing a shotgun at my two friends and coworkers, our respective dogs flanking her sides and front on the defense.

"Easy, Xena," I said soothingly, wrapping one arm around her waist, bringing her back into my body, then grabbing the rifle, waiting for her to let go of it so I could set it against the porch railing, before surrounding her waist with that one as well. "Off, Renegade."

The men chuckled lowly, but I could tell Aspen wasn't pleased with the groan she emitted.

I winced as soon as I saw Rex's face.

"Fucking bear got me, man," he said.

I smirked. "Uh-huh. Nice stitchwork."

"Just another scar for the beard to cover when it grows back," he responded, rubbing at his missing facial hair, unperturbed.

I understood why Aspen was standoffish, especially when it came to Rex. With the angry scar around his jugular, and the stitches currently covering nearly his entire cheek on the right side of his face, he surely didn't look like a savory character.

"You alright there, Cade?" Dalton asked.

"Concussion and banged up, but still alive thanks to this lady, here," I said, then released Aspen from my grip, coming forward toward the steps and shaking each man's hand. "Pen, I believe we talked about these two goofs last night."

She nodded, a little shell-shocked I was sure, but then came forward, presenting her hand. "Sorry about the firepower."

"No worries." Rex's smirk looked more like a grimace. "You can never be too careful out here."

"I've been greeted with worse," Dalton chuckled, then winked at me. "Thanks for saving our guy here."

"You're welcome." It sounded more like a question, then she turned to me. "I guess you're leaving?"

She was right.

I was.

But I didn't want to go just yet.

"What about my truck?" I asked, effectively stalling my departure, giving Aspen my answer.

"Dropped Babyface off to take it back," Dalton explained, then he tossed me what looked like a new phone. "He told us to give you this. Same number as before. Contacts and previous information's been migrated over. We realized yours was dead as soon as we couldn't get a location on you."

Right. That fucking GPS tracker. I had a new appreciation for our computer geek, no matter that his gadget hadn't saved me this time around, or his annoying habit of gifting us with our personalized ringtones.

"So how'd you find him then?" Aspen asked.

"Our tech guy, Bryce that is, pulled a GPS map of Cade's phone's last pinged coordinates," he explained. "Then again, we already knew the general vicinity once Rex told us where he was attacked, hunting down a skip."

"And the body?" she asked.

"Handled. Our buddy, Shane, is a detective with the Jacksonville PD," Dalton explained.

One look in Aspen's direction and I could tell she was enthralled with all this information coming from them. A laugh broke loose from me as urged Dalton to continue with a, "Go on."

"Well," he began, eyeing me with curiosity. "That's it."

Rex shrugged at his side, confirming what D said.

"That's it?" she asked, clearly disappointed. "That's kind of anti-climactic."

"Why is that?" Rex asked, brows furrowed as he crossed his arms over his broad chest.

"Well, Cade painted you guys as a bunch of *G.I. Joe* badasses, running around saving people for a price. I've always been fascinated about that whole computer, techie, hacking kind of thing. In fact, I've been thinking about writing—"

The confused looks from both Rex and Dalton had me covering Aspen's mouth with a chuckle.

"Rex, this'll most likely fly ten feet over your head, but D, I believe you'll recognize the name Penny Sexton?" I said, then gently let my hand fall away from Aspen's mouth.

It took a moment for the name to register with the man, but when it did, his eyes widened.

"The writer?" Rex blurted before my part-time boss had a chance to say anything.

Say what?

"The fuck?" Dalton asked, then turned to our partner.

He shrugged. "Her motorcycle club series kicks ass. And don't get me started on the sex scenes."

The blush on her face flew straight past her cheeks, flourishing up to her hairline, which had me laughing once more.

"Wait until I tell Dev about this," Dalton grinned. "She's gonna flip her lid."

"She'll set her hacker ways to work and hunt the poor woman down. Don't do it," Rex said with a vehement shake of the head, his eyes having gone wide.

Aspen perked up. "Did you say, *hacker*?"

"Guys, I think you're flipping her out," I said, looking to the woman in question out of concern.

"Not at all," she said, shaking her head vehemently. "Do you think I could get in touch with her? Strictly for educational purposes of course."

Right.

And one day pigs would fly.

Call me crazy, but I had a feeling once I left Aspen's cottage, it wouldn't be the last I saw of her.

I sure as fuck hoped it wouldn't be.

eight

MOLLY SIMPLY WASN'T the same the week after Cade and Renegade left. I had to smile at the memory of that day though, because it didn't look as though Renegade had wanted to leave either. As for the man himself, I could tell he was itching to get back to normalcy, whatever that might be; even if I could have sworn he'd been a little reluctant to say goodbye too. That was most likely due to my hopeless romantic imagination though.

Early in the mornings, however, instead of sleeping in like was my normal, I'd found myself lying awake, wrapped in loads of blankets so I could cut the chill of the room.

Hell, I'd even started stacking pillows directly behind me before falling asleep, only to find them tossed off the bed haphazardly and no sense of security or comfort offered. It sucked that this chaos had come about after a single night of being cuddled. I could only imagine how bereft I'd have felt had Cade stayed longer.

Let's be honest here, I missed him.

Albert Caden Summers—the book thief.

And he was technically nothing but a stranger, one who I'd gotten to know over the course of two days since the first of his seventy-two-hour stay had been ones he'd spent unconscious in my bed, with me ogling him like some silly schoolgirl with a crush.

Cue my sigh.

He was an incredible specimen of a man; one I found myself tied to since my childhood, and I must confess, I was undoubtedly curious to know more about him too.

Groaning, I peered at the clock, only for it to reveal it was barely six in the morning. Figuring it was going to be a day of burning through one cup of coffee after another, I dragged my ass out of bed and headed toward the bedroom door.

"Molly?" I called out, noticing she wasn't at the foot of the bed or in my room for that matter.

Nothing but a loud doggy sigh came from the direction of the front door.

Poor pup. She missed her companion worse than I missed his owner.

Another three weeks went by, and I couldn't seem to focus much on my latest book, so I was glad when Molly's annual vet checkup came around the corner. There'd been far too many odd happenings concerning my dog and my house as of late, and I was starting to worry about the number of shredded blankets and pieces of clothing I was finding in random corners of my home. Never in the five years since I'd brought her home had my girl done that.

As much as I preferred being alone, there were times where I thrived within the public—usually as Penny Sexton, but today, the world would have to deal with Aspen Ridge—one who was feeling a little antsy within the four walls of her cottage as of late.

Eyeing the business card Cade's partner/boss had left me when I'd mentioned I'd like to talk to Devolin, his woman as he so eloquently put it, I began to wonder if inspiration could perhaps come out of a visit with her—maybe her insight would knock me back into a productive writing mode.

With said card tucked in my wallet, I grabbed Molly's leash and we headed for the front door.

"What do you mean *pregnant*?"

There's no way I heard the octogenarian in front of me right.

And seven pups?

Seven!

"She's about a month in, now," Dr. Feinstein added on an excited nod.

"But how?" The remainder of my words froze in my mouth as realization hit.

Renegade. Fucking mangy, protective mutt!

Seven!

Fuck!

Shit!

Damn!

"W—when is she due?" I had to deal with this newfound reality of mine. How the hell was I going to handle this many pups? I had no room for that large of a litter. Hell, it had been cramped with Renegade and Cade inside my small cottage with us both; and don't get me started on what I needed to do to assist her with birthing those pups.

What if she has complications? What if she lost the litter? What if—

"From her ultrasound, I'd say you've got about thirty days, give or take a week, before these little critters come out to play," he smiled. "Normal gestation period is about sixty-three days."

He's kidding, right? Please tell me I'm dreaming!

Yet part of my heart fluttered with excitement as I looked at Molly lying relaxed at my feet, contentment emanating from my fur baby.

"Hussy," I muttered. "Why'd you have to go and make me a grandma in my mid-thirties, huh?" Her entire back end wiggled in excitement as she tilted her chin up at me. Grabbing her leash, I thanked the doctor, then left the room to pay at the reception counter. "I don't care how cute they are, you can't keep them all," I told her as she eyed me with...was that a twinkle of pride or plea in her eyes?

Okay...maybe just one.

Damn, I'm such a pushover, but it sure explained the cloth shredding. My pooch was nesting.

CADE

The knock on my front door had me smiling.

It meant one thing: food.

Renegade's incessant barking at said door though, had me groaning.

"Pipe down, Ren," I ordered. I could have sworn the dog rolled his eyes at me as I grabbed my wallet and headed for the entrance. "Renegade, hush!" No go.

Frustrated with the canine's recent tendency to ignore my commands—it had been like this since we'd left Aspen's woodsy cottage—I opened the door as I fished around for the right amount of cash, then handed it to the delivery kid without looking up.

"Renegade! Bad boy!" was my greeting, followed promptly by a furball racing past my legs and almost bowling me over. "Molly, get back here!"

"Aspen," rushed through my lips in a single breath.

Both of us stared at one another, flabbergasted by the play of events before us, and I found myself getting lost in those bright emeralds of hers.

But not for long.

"Renegade, back!" the woman before me bellowed, then pushed past me as I stood there dumbstruck.

On a whine, I didn't have to look back to know that my dog had listened to her with much dismay.

"Why are you yelling at my dog?" I asked, turning to face her and the canine commotion after I'd closed the door.

Her arm shot out, index finger aimed at Renegade. "Your damn mutt got mine knocked up!" she shouted.

I turned to look at the two canines, already cuddled up with one another, paying us no attention whatsoever.

Huh!

"Do you know how to deal with birthing a litter? And what the hell is whelping? Or how about dealing with training or ensuring the safety of the seven pups about to shoot out of my baby girl in approximately thirty days?" Her perplexed look had me fighting the urge to bust a gut laughing, so instead, I stepped toward her and grabbed her forearms in my hands, pulling her forward so we stood toe to toe. "I'm not ready to be a grandma, Cade, and it's all your fault!" Rant over, her head thumped my shoulder; defeated by life's circumstances.

She was out of steam.

Then I chose that moment to burst out laughing.

"Puppies are cute," is what came next, then I wrapped my arms around her, crushing her to me in what I hoped was a soothing hug.

"Seven," is her mumbled rebuttal. "And you stole my book."

Seven? My body stiffened.

"That's right, mister; and I'm not doing this by myself either," she declared, pushing back from me before poking me in my chest, and gracing me with that fiery gaze of hers I'd missed since I'd left her on her front porch. "Your dog is half the problem, so you're going to be half of the solution, you hear me?"

Fuck, but she'd only gotten hotter in the month since I'd last seen her. My dreams surely hadn't done her justice. Those eyes...that flush in her cheeks...those pink kissable—

Focus.

"Cade, did you hear me—"

Nah.

With one step toward her, I smashed my lips down on hers, and took what I'd been craving since that morning I'd woken up with her in my arms, what felt like a lifetime ago.

That's when the doorbell rang.

For once, I wasn't smiling at the idea of food. In fact, I groaned as I pulled away, my mind reeling, but my stomach rumbling its hunger, despite my cock telling me it was hungry for something entirely different. Hell, I barely felt the light thumping—a residual thing left over from my moderate concussion, according to the doctors I'd seen—in my head.

"This is far from over," I vowed not only to myself, but to Aspen as my thumb skimmed her swollen lips.

Ignoring the glowing flush, her heavy breathing, and those addictive lips of hers, I turned for the door. I took the pizza from the kid's arms, shoved the bills that most likely would cover three of those pies, and received a "Sorry, man," as I slammed the door in the acne-ridden pubescent's face.

It wasn't until I'd turned toward my unannounced guest

that I spotted her blush, then followed her eyes down to my crotch.

Great, caught again.

Shrugging off my wayward dick's reaction—which had a tendency of standing at attention every time I seemed to think about the Amazon standing in my living room—I made my way toward my kitchen. "Come on. You're staying for dinner."

"I can't," Aspen said.

"You can, and you will."

"I have to be getting back before it gets too late to drive. You saw how narrow those roads are."

"Then if it's too late, you'll stay the night," I told her. "It's the least I can do. And don't worry, I have a spare room you can crash in."

Feet shuffled in behind me, then stopped.

"What the hell?" I heard.

Ah! She'd found it.

Settling the pizza box on the counter, I pulled out an extra plate and glasses from the cabinet, then served up a large slice for each of us. Aspen's eyes were on me the minute I walked back out to the living room with our meal, then followed me as I returned with napkins and our glasses of water.

"You bought my books?" she asked, as I settled myself down on the couch.

"Mmm." I lifted my plate and slice toward my mouth. I had purchased all of them and the three currently on preorder as a matter-of-fact.

"You have a library?" she continued as I took a bite.

"Mm-hmm," came mumbled over the stringy cheese goodness.

"You've read all of these?"

I swallowed. "Yup," I popped the 'P.' "Some of them more than once or twice. Now come on, your dinner is getting cold."

On a huff, she did as I asked and dug in, even though I could tell she was chomping at the bit to figure me out some more. With my faculties fully intact however, I was going to make it a bit more challenging for the woman this time around. She'd have to give me some of herself before I gave her more of me.

Halfway through her first slice, the dam burst, and the inquisition recommenced.

"Have you read any more of mine, aside from the one you started at my cottage? By the way, I want that copy back."

"About half of them so far, but I think your favorite is mine too," I announced. "So when's *Sheltered Love* coming out?" I already knew the answer, but I didn't want her to think I'd become obsessed with all things about her, especially her work, because it had been the only thing readily available to me. I'd once heard inside an author's mind there was always a bit of truth to what they wrote. Whether it be fantasy or experience, it was part of their makeup. I have to say, based on her erotic writing, I'd become a little more than curious.

"In a few months."

"Good."

"Good? That's all?"

"Yeah, that's all," I parroted. "For a woman with a lost faith in Search and Rescue, I have to say I'm impressed on how likeable you've made the hero. I want to know what happens next between those two."

"Hmm." Aspen set her empty plate down on the coffee table.

"Another?" When she nodded, I grabbed her plate and mine, and headed toward the kitchen once more. "I meant to ask if you wanted something other than water earlier, but you were a little distracted. I've got beer, white wine, iced tea, and—"

"Beer." Her reply made me jump because, unbeknownst to me, Aspen had followed in behind. "I'll get those, if you're okay with that."

"Thanks," I mumbled, then headed toward the living room with our second helpings.

nine

I CAN'T BELIEVE I'd given in to Cade's demands that I stay the night, but the flutter of anticipation deep inside my belly and the little devil on my shoulder, dancing with excitement, had me forgetting my obligations.

What obligations?

True. I'd fed the chickens. The house was clean within an inch of my life; any cleaner and it would have rivaled the best hospital in our area. For once, I wasn't hearing Molly whining around the clock, and I hadn't had to cook for myself.

How long has it been since I had a pizza this good?

Not finishing my third slice, feeling as though I was ready to burst, I set my piece of pizza down and got up to inspect Cade's bookshelves a bit more closely.

Patterson.

Rice.

Dickens.

Poe.

Some nonfiction works based on world history, criminology, and even healthcare.

Then there's little ol' me thrown into the mix alongside some of my romantic suspense idols.

"This is quite the collection," I said more to myself than to my host.

"I like things quiet," he responded, making me jump. I hadn't heard him get up and move toward me. "Whenever I have free time, I like to chill with a good book. Renegade appreciates the rest too. Between my day job and helping the guys at Nightshade, we haven't had much downtime, except for recently. The doc told me I had a moderate concussion. I've been off of work until this past week."

"Hmm. I'm glad you're okay."

Suddenly, his arms were surrounding me, the warmth of his chest seeping into my back. "Now what's this about me owing you a book?"

Oh, right.

"You took that copy of *Sheltered Rescue* you were reading when you left my place," I said.

"No, I didn't." Turning on him, I'd suspected he'd loosen his hold, but he didn't. His face displayed his confusion. "I put it back on your shelf next to the others before I got gone."

"You did?" I whispered, but somehow, I just knew he was telling the truth, with the intense look of sincerity in his eyes. "But it's not there." Instead, I shook my head, more of a way to get myself out of this trancelike sensation that was setting in, and said, "Maybe I just misplaced it. I am working on the follow-up to it after all, and I must have grabbed it and forgotten about it." But even as I said it, I knew it wasn't the case. I never misplaced my books, which led me to wonder where it could have gone.

"You sure?" I could feel his deep rasp through his chest, soaking into mine as his face grew nearer.

"Mm-hmm."

Then his lips captured mine, demanding more from me than when I'd first showed up on his doorstep.

Now, I might be a bit on the inexperienced side, but I'm no nun. Cade's lips were made to sin, and those unholy talents of his had me at their mercy.

With a simple kiss, one he took his time with, I found myself wanting to peel every stitch of clothing off, lie down on the nearest flat surface, and offer myself up to the man pressed against me. Instead, my rational self kicked in and I pushed him away.

"What'd you do that for?" I huffed out through heavy breaths, instantly hating myself for the look of rejection I spotted in his features.

As quick as I'd seen it, he replaced the expression with a small smirk. "Didn't I tell you earlier that we weren't done?"

Call me crazy, but the self-assuredness he displayed was charming more than it was asshole-ish in nature.

"We're done for now," I spat, trying to break his hold on me, but he didn't let go.

"I can't stop thinking about you, Aspen," he whispered.

"Stockholm," I blurted.

His laugh was short and lacked hilarity. "Doubt it."

His arms fell away from me and I felt the loss of his heat immediately.

I shrugged. "You were in duress. It makes sense." Turning away from him, I stepped to the side, making my way toward the couch, where I dropped onto the cushions and proceeded to chug the rest of the beer I'd been drinking.

"Another?" he offered with what sounded like humor in his tone.

I couldn't look him in the eyes. "Better not."

"Afraid you'll lose control?" he pushed.

Maybe. But I chose to lead with, "Not in the least," and straightened my posture to project as much confidence I knew I wasn't feeling right then, meeting his eyes to punctuate my meaning.

"Suit yourself, then," he said, then headed for the fridge as Molly lifted her head to look at me and huffed what seemed like annoyance at my stubbornness before settling in to Renegade's side once more.

My own dog had my number. Jeez, was I that transparent?

CADE

I knew she'd said no to the drink, but her eyes had said yes, and seeing as I felt overwhelmed by the sparks that flew during that kiss, I figured instead of mauling her, I could at least indulge one of her wants, even though she'd refused it.

Popping the cap off two bottles of the brew I had in stock, I took a deep breath, reliving the moment I got a real good taste of Aspen Ridge.

Beer and woman.

Soft and warm.

She'd melted into my hold, giving as much as she got in those swift few moments, and I now found myself pitching a tent in my jeans for the umpteenth time at the mere thought of her. And I knew it wouldn't end there either.

Get yourself under control, Summers.

With things finally beginning to deflate down there, I headed back to the living room, only to find the woman I'd been enthralled with, for the better part of the last month, cuddled up with Renegade and Molly on the floor.

"I still can't believe he knocked her up," she muttered, then accepted the beer I held out for her without hesitation. "And I see I am as transparent as Molly has led me to believe."

"How long now?" I asked, choosing not to comment on how easy she'd been to read, then I parked my ass on the edge of my coffee table just so I could be close to her.

"Thirty days or so. She's practically halfway there already and I had no clue," Aspen pouted. "I feel like I've failed at being a good doggy parent."

"Don't feel bad," I said. "I never thought twice about what could happen. Ren never got fixed because working dogs seem to do their job better when everything is..." I searched for the best word to talk about my dog's junk.

"Intact?" Aspen provided with a laughing tone.

I nodded my response, observing her with the furry couple as I took a sip of my beer. No matter how pissed off she seemed to be when she'd first arrived, she was showering as much attention on Renegade as she was Molly, and both canines were soaking it all up.

"Are you ready to be a daddy?" she cooed to my partner.

I swear Renegade lifted his head with excited eyes and nodded before sneaking a lick at her hand, then at Molly's snout.

"I hope Grandpa over there is ready for furry trouble."

That got my attention. "Who, me?"

She smirked. "Yes, *Grandpa*."

"Why can't I be the cool uncle?" I asked, not really liking the title that suddenly made me feel old beyond my years.

"Because you're his owner," she giggled, "and if I'm being labeled as Grandma, I'm sure as hell not going down with that title on my own."

I laughed along with her, then thought about what all of

this entailed, and I found myself discovering how Aspen must have felt when she first discovered the news. Anxiety hit me.

"What the fuck are we going to do with seven pups?"

She bit her lip, then whispered, "I don't know." Her hand buried itself in the fur behind Molly's ear. "I feel sad giving them up, but it's unrealistic to keep them all, you know?"

"Mm-hmm." My mind was reeling with possibilities however, but I wanted to think on things before suggesting anything to the woman seated across from me. I had less than thirty days to figure out my plan, then propose—a solution that is.

ten

Aspen

TALK about a bad time to leave my laptop in the car.

It was well past midnight and approximately two hours since Cade and I had each gone our respective ways—to bed as it were—and I still hadn't managed to fall asleep.

Ideas were flooding my mind and I had nothing but my phone to log where I would take my characters next.

It's better than nothing.

I sighed.

Molly had ditched me for Renegade, and being set up in a strange bed that smelled like the man I'd been missing over the last month—without said man—wasn't helping my sleepless status.

Getting up, I figured I might as well be productive. I tiptoed to the front door, unlocking it as I slid on my shoes, then reached for the knob.

A shrill sound scared the shit out of me, causing me to slam the front door shut as both dogs barked furiously.

"What the fuck?" Cade came out, rubbing at his eyes,

sporting nothing but a pair of very tight boxer briefs that left nothing to the imagination.

Here I was, running shoes on, in nothing but a pair of too-big shorts—curtesy of the man of the house himself—and my next-to-nothing tank top, which had been under my sweater earlier; sans bra no less.

I felt like a teenager caught sneaking out of the house after curfew, or rather, what I thought it would feel like since I'd never really tested that theory or acquired that particular badge of honor.

Within seconds, Cade was at a control panel next to the door, breathing heavily as he hit a series of buttons.

Ah, sweet silence.

"What the fuck do you think you're doing?" he barked through the ongoing ringing in my ears.

My eyes widened and my brows knitted. He looked pissed. "I-I... I couldn't sleep."

His brows furrowed with incredulity. "You couldn't sleep?"

"I thought I'd write," I explained further.

"You thought you would write?" he parroted again, this time, his voice a little softer. Maybe he wasn't ticked at me.

"I needed my laptop."

"Mm-hmm." His eyes were cast downward at my tits, but I couldn't move to even cover myself, frozen at his shameless interest and not knowing where his mood would take us next.

"I left it in my car," I whispered, my body heating; my nipples standing at attention.

He licked his lips, an obvious sign of arousal mixed with perhaps a smidgen of annoyance. "I see," he said roughly.

"I couldn't sleep," I repeated dumbly, too flustered to make out where this conversation was headed.

His eyes darted to mine as he swallowed hard, then extended his hand. "Keys."

"Huh?"

He cleared his throat. "Give me your keys."

"O—okay." I dropped them into his waiting hand and jumped back a step just as immediately.

It took him thirty or so seconds—I didn't really count—before he was out the door, barefoot and relatively naked, then back with my laptop bag in tow and the door was being locked once more.

As he reactivated the house alarm, I found my eyes fused to his back, moving lower. It was easier doing the perusing than being subjected to his perusal: muscles, tattoos, rippling of arms, firm ass. It wasn't until his throat cleared that my eyes diverted from their feasting, at which point I realized were directly aimed at his growing cock.

Busted!

"Sweetheart, keep eyeing me like that and you can forget writing, or going back to bed for that matter."

"Huh?"

"You make it hard to keep my hands off you, Pen," he rasped.

"I'm sorry?" My body flushed with heat once more, my nipples which had started to go down, became erect again, and I swear I might have mini-orgasmed from the heat in his gaze.

Setting my laptop bag down, he dropped my keys on to the table by the front entrance, then stepped toward me. I moved back as he matched me step for step until my backside came flush with the wall.

"You're not sorry at all, sweetheart," he whispered, his eyes studying mine. One hand braced him against the wall, while the other came down to play with a loose strand of my hair, tucking it behind my ear.

"Cade," I breathed as his face came nearer.

"Pen," I felt more than heard over my lips.

His lips took mine, hungry and animalistic, and I had to brace. Of course, all I had to hold on to was the large bicep by my head and Cade's shirt. Wait...there was no shirt. His chest. His wonderfully warm and smooth chest, speckled with just enough hair that if my boobs were uncovered, they'd enjoy the delicious friction provided.

My thoughts had me moaning, thus opening for his assault, and what an attack it was. Warm and sweet; tasting of toothpaste and man. I'd never wanted more from the opposite sex than right then.

Before I knew it, Cade had picked me up, guided me so I would wrap my legs around his waist as he pressed me farther into the wall, which forced me to grab on to his shoulders for stability.

Now, I'd written scenes like this before, but holy shit! I'll admit, I thought they were hot when I wrote them, but they'd never do the real thing justice. I'm talking singe the hairs off your arms, melt the toughest of metals *hot*!

Just as I thought he'd move us to the nearest horizontal surface and have his way with me, his kisses slowed to a complete halt.

Forehead to forehead, his breathing was labored, and I leaned in for more, letting him know I was more than fine with where things between us were headed.

"Shit, Pen," he growled as he met me peck for peck. "This isn't what I planned."

I pulled back slightly. "Cade..." I grabbed on to the sides of his face, my thumbs rubbing his jaw, which carried a scruff I had reveled in only seconds before as it abraded the skin of my face. "It's okay."

He squeezed my ass before he set me down, leaning his head on my shoulder, causing me to drop my arms at my sides. "I didn't mean to maul you like that," he explained. "It's just..."

I tried calming my racing heart. "I get it." I swallowed hard. "I really do. It's not me, it's—"

His head snapped upright, then stepping back, he stared me down. "Are you fucking kidding me?"

My mouth went dry at the rippling of solid muscles in his torso. "What?"

"Don't give me that *it's not you, it's me bullshit*, sweetheart." His eyes had me pinned to where I stood. "I don't work that way. If I'm attracted to someone, I let them know. And in case you missed it," he looked down at his crotch, "I'm attracted to you, Aspen Ridge, unbelievably so. I'm simply trying to say I shouldn't have gone at you like I did."

So much for calm breathing. Hell, forget breathing at all. "W —why not? What's the problem then?"

"A few kisses here and there is one thing. Dry humping against my fucking wall is another," he said, closing the distance between us. Grabbing on to the sides of my neck, he tilted my head back enough so he could kiss my forehead. "I want to know more about you. I want to take you out. I want to see how excited you get when you meet Devolin for the first time; and be there when you put those puzzle pieces together to write your next bestseller. I want us to date, and yes...I want us to fuck." I couldn't help the giggle that escaped, which netted me with a chaste kiss on the mouth. "Fuck, you're sexy as all hell, woman, and when you get mad or defensive, I love that the fire in your eyes matches your hair. When you're turned on, you melt for me. I want to see that and know every little nuance of you in between."

Holy shit!

"Are you for real?" I blinked, thinking that maybe I had fallen asleep and this whole scenario was in my dreams.

A puff of laughter followed and a light pinch to my backside had me jumping. "It's real, sweetheart, and just so you know, you're not going to be writing tonight." With what seemed like an all too effortless lift, Caden Summers had me in his arms and was walking us toward his bedroom. Renegade graced us with a bark of approval before settling down next to his mate.

CADE

I've never felt a state of panic so severe until my home's alarm went off twenty minutes ago. Thank fuck I got to it in time before Dalton and his crew called things in. I wouldn't put it past Brycen to have tapped into the video portion of my security system and noticed that my visitor had spent the night, which is why I hurried my ass out the door, waved at the camera hidden in a corner by my front entrance, and hustled to get Aspen's laptop bag back to her. There's no fucking way I was going to let her out the door in that barely-there tank top with those tight as fuck nipples on display. If anyone saw those at all, it would be me and me alone.

"What's with the growl?" Aspen asked, as I set her down on my mattress, then she jolted to sit upright. "Oh shit, did I hurt you? I knew I shouldn't have let you—"

"Simmer down," I nervously laughed off my sudden sense of possessiveness. "I was just thinking I forgot the light on in the entranceway and instead of getting in bed with you right this second like I'm dying to, I need to go turn it off."

Yeah. Right. That was it. Well, it was, but I wasn't going to tell her the truth of where my mind had wandered off to. To be honest, I didn't give a rat's ass about the fucking lights. If she knew the truth of how I already viewed her as mine and only mine, she'd probably run out of here like her hair had caught fire.

Another one of those giggles came, making my dick take notice.

"Hurry back," she said, smiling as she threw herself onto the pillows.

By the time I'd checked the house's surroundings, looked in on the dogs, turned all unnecessary lights off, and made my way back to my bedroom, Aspen was fast asleep, snoring lightly with her arms wrapped around my pillow, her head cocooned by the padded cotton of the one on her side of the bed.

Softly dropping to the mattress, I shuffled my body as close as I could get to Aspen's, then wrestled my pillow from her arms, tucking it haphazardly behind my head, and settled in.

"Much better," Aspen mumbled before snuggling closer, letting me get my arm under her, then emitting another cute snore.

"Definitely," I whispered mostly to myself, as I buffed my cheek against the top of her head, hugging her to my side.

eleven

IT MIGHT NOT HAVE BEEN the night I'd envisioned, but it was a night worth waking from with the contented feeling I was graced with.

Wrapped around me like some spider monkey, Aspen had finally quit flopping like a fish out of water around three. It had taken some work, but once I'd wrapped myself around her, she had settled. It seemed the more secure of a hold I had on the woman, the less she moved around. Just as well; I had yet to find a member of the opposite sex who enjoyed being held and did some holding of her own right back as we lay together. To be honest, I slept better that way too.

A foot made its way up my calf, between my legs, so I gave Aspen a squeeze to let her know I was coherent and jokingly added, "You're not going to run off for the bathroom first thing, are you?"

A snort. "You're in luck," she announced, then burrowed deeper into my side, tucking her head into my neck so her nose nuzzled my chin.

"Sleep well?" I asked.

"Yes. Thank you. I haven't slept this well in...well, since you were..."

"Me neither," I confessed, giving her a squeeze before my hugging arm set forth with a soothing pattern over her shoulder and arm.

Minutes were filled with silence, but none of it was awkward, until the woman lying in my arms shifted.

"Is this weird?" she asked.

"What do you mean?"

"This. *Us*. How fast this happened?" Her hand waved between us, her gaze fastened to my chin instead of looking into my eyes.

"You mean how quick I was to maul you, then bring you to my bed, where I left you for a few minutes, came back, and you were sawin' logs?"

She slapped my chest, making me laugh, then rolled onto her back, covering her face with her forearm. "Ugh."

I rolled to a hover above her. "It's okay, Pen." I kissed her open palm. "We might have fooled around." I kissed the pulse point on her wrist, then nipped it, causing her body to quake with a shiver, then I shifted her arm above her head and held it there loosely so she could free it if she felt the need to. She didn't.

"Cade." She swallowed hard, her green eyes growing bright.

"As I've observed in the short time we've known each other, we wouldn't be us if someone or something didn't get in our way during those times," I explained.

And right then, my phone rang with an incoming call.

Fucking Murphy! I thought about the law that seemed to dominate all the intimate interactions we've had thus far.

Anticipation gave way to humored curiosity as Aspen's

brow arched and her body shook with silent giggles. "*North Woods Law*?"

Dropping my head to her collarbone on a sigh, I groaned as I pushed up and sat on the edge of the bed. "We'll talk about how you know that when I'm done with Bryce, seeing as I know you don't have a television."

"I've got internet most of the time," she explained. "Who's Bryce?"

"Brycen. He's one of the guys at Nightshade." I grabbed my phone from the nightstand and thumbed to the right to accept the call. "Yeah, Babyface?" The grin I has when Aspen snorted a laugh was short lived.

"We need you."

I turned to look at a relaxed Aspen watching me, and a sense of disappointment hit me square in the chest. "Right now?"

"D's got a lead on that missing kid and doesn't want to waste time," he said. I couldn't blame Dalton for his take on this particular case. "Expect to be gone a few days."

"Renegade?" I asked.

"No need this time around. They have their own hounds."

"You're gonna have to give me some time to find—"

Aspen's warm hand landed on my bicep, turning my focus back toward her. She wore a look of understanding. "I'll look after him if you need someone."

"Bryce, hold on a sec." I muted my phone. "You sure? It wouldn't be for more than a few days."

She shook her head. "Take as long as you need. It'll be nice to have Molly behaving more like herself for a while. I think she missed Renegade more than I thought."

I missed you too, I thought.

And I knew I'd miss her some more while I was away on business.

"You're sure?" I asked again, as I heard Brycen on the other end of the line say, "Yo!"

"Definitely." She punctuated her answer with a huge grin.

I hit the button to unmute my phone. "Bryce? It's a go. Tell the boss man I'll be at headquarters in a little over an hour and I expect the entire file and a full debrief when I get there."

"Roger that." With no more fanfare, the man hung up and I dropped my phone onto the nightstand before letting myself collapse backward, my head landing on Aspen's belly.

"I didn't mean to eavesdrop," she whispered, her hand mindlessly playing through my disheveled hair.

"I've nothing to hide from you, Pen," I said, then turned, pushing myself up before crawling overtop of her, and settling myself down over her sleep-warmed body, cradling her legs between mine.

"Cade—"

I shook my head to stop her words. "Nothing to hide." I held her eyes with intensity to make my point clear, until she offered me a small nod of capitulation.

"We should talk about Renegade," she whispered, which caused my gaze to shift to her lips, giving me all sorts of ideas; ones I was going to follow through with someday soon. It wasn't like she didn't know how to handle or take care of my dog. She had her own after all.

"Later." My voice sounded like gravel, then I leaned down to taste her mouth briefly before adding, "Just five more minutes."

Leaning up, her arms wrapped themselves around my shoulders and her mouth connected with mine.

Glad we're on the same page.

ASPEN

Five minutes turned into ten, then fifteen, until we'd hit the twenty-minute mark and the urge to do more than simple dry-humping over our underwear had become overwhelming.

If I wasn't careful, I could get lost in a man like Caden Summers.

You can't.

But it would be so great if I could. He was sweet, caring, attentive, and all man. And he was clear with the fact he wanted me. That shotgun in his tight briefs couldn't lie; and his eyes...those eyes only spoke the truth, his body enunciated it, and his mouth...

"We can't keep doing this," he pecked me on the mouth, "or else I won't leave." Another peck, this time over one eye. "And I really don't want to leave you like this," he nibbled at my jaw and continued, "wanting and unsatisfied."

I didn't want it to end that way either, but on a sigh, I agreed half-heartedly. "We should get up."

A horn blared at me before a car blazed past, just shy of five minutes of leaving Cade's house.

After loading up my Jeep with Renegade's toys and food, even his favorite bed, the man of the house had pushed me against the side of my ride, then proceeded to kiss me dizzy, as if he was making love to my mouth.

Hell, it's all I've been able to think about since I'd left his place; hence why my current driving tactics resembled that of an eighty-year-old lady's snail speed.

Checking my mirror to peer into the back seat, Molly and her man were cuddled comfortably across the bench. Looking at Renegade, a dog who most definitely mirrored his owner in personality, I knew I was in trouble.

twelve

CADE

MY GO BAG was in the back, and I'd just left NSI's headquarters for the South Carolina border.

Amanda 'Nikki' Camp had been last seen, by a bystander, in the back seat of a white Honda Civic at a Jacksonville 7-Eleven on Bell Fork Road, a little over three weeks ago. Now that the same car had been found abandoned and burned to a crisp on an old gravel road outside of Monroe, the smoke having attracted the attention of civilians who called in emergency crews, it was all hands on deck.

This is where I came in.

I hated cases like this the most: the ones where it was likely the victim's parents and family would be receiving tragic news. Then again, I suppose, in this particular case, the tragic news could potentially be doubled considering the mother's brother had been the one who'd taken off with the seven-year-old girl.

The situation made my mind wander to Aspen's past and what she had been through as a child, losing her sister like she had. Being the only witness, ridiculed beyond reprieve, had been tough on her. She didn't have to tell me this as I'd seen it with my own two eyes as a schoolmate of hers and then again, when she'd reiterated her version of what she'd been through, that one night in her bed. In truth, every missing child case like this had me thinking of the one case my father—rest his soul—had never been able to solve.

On top of work, our morning tryst in bed after Brycen had called me, followed with that hot goodbye kiss against Aspen's car, had my mind reeling. I wanted this assignment to be done and over with, and for the girl's family to get their closure, so I could get back to my woman—yes, she was mine, whether she knew it or not—and our dogs, and finish what we'd started.

But first thing's first. I needed to connect with the FBI contact Dalton had provided me once I got to Monroe.

We were too late. I just knew it.

Dereck Elliott had been located, half a mile from his burned-out car, hanging on by a slim thread. He was on route to the nearest hospital, an FBI team of agents on their tail after he'd nearly been taken out by part of his own vehicle, which blew up when the engine had exploded.

"No sign of the girl," Agent Langley told me what I'd pretty much assumed.

"Could have used Renegade," I mumbled.

"Your canine partner?" she asked, to which I nodded. "We have our own which is why we didn't request him."

"That's fine," I smirked. "I have a feeling he's happier with his mate at home."

She snorted. "Nice." Looking into the trees, she took a long inhale, then released it, regaining her focus. "Something tells me she's in this area. I hope I'm right."

I had the same feeling; hence it was why—within the next

few hours—we had a search party put together with the FBI's canine unit, in order to cover the most ground before darkness fell. Time was of the essence when someone was lost and exposed to the elements.

"Team Tango coming in. Got something northeast of the burn site," came crackling from the radio approximately four hours later.

"How far, Tango?" Langley demanded from our command post.

To be honest, I'd have rather gone ahead and joined the search, but with my First Responder training, I understood they needed me on standby for this particular case. Let's face it, this was an FBI investigation after all, with cooperation from various local police detachments. Where I was concerned, when Dalton owes someone, he comes through, and the way he does that is he sends the best man for the job he's got on hand; and this time, it was me.

"Twelve miles out," came crackling back.

That far? "Coordinates?"

Langley radioed Tango with my inquiry as I grabbed the pack I had brought with me, hitched it onto my back, and finished preparing to leave, albeit grabbing my own radio and tuning it to the team's frequency.

"Testing," I said into my radio, as I walked far enough away from Langley to ensure proper connection. "Summers to command post, over."

"Testing loud and clear," came back.

"Tango, ready when needed," I radioed. "What you got?"

"Shoe," the voice mumbled. "We're still looking—" My heart bottomed out. "Ah, fuck."

"Command to Tango, SITREP!" Langley barked, as anxious

as I was to get the situation report from the team, but I already knew it wouldn't be good.

"Found her," came next, sounding painful even to my ears. "Alive, but barely."

My hand came up to my mouth as my thumb pressed the *call* button, and before I'd uttered, "Rescue on the move, over," my feet had already broken through the edge of the forest, the coordinates I'd entered in my handheld GPS already telling me I was heading in the right direction. So long as the terrain wasn't too rough or dense to navigate, it would take the average person about two hours to make it there. I aimed to cut that down to half of that if I could, all the while checking in with Langley at base and Tango at the scene, providing them pointers on how to help the victim until I got to her.

ASPEN

I might not have a TV, but that didn't mean I didn't have the capability to stream live programing when the mood struck me.

On the first night, after Cade had left Renegade in my care, I found myself daydreaming about him and not being productive in the least with the chapter I was trying to write. The only reason I didn't feel the pressure was mostly because I'd given my editor more than what had been asked of me last week so she wouldn't hound me until closer to the end of this week for more.

As it was, I found myself on a local news channel site I visited regularly, checking out what was going on beyond my quiet little corner of the world. My fingers stopped dead in their tracks and my eyes widened on a kidnapping article.

Right in front of me was a photo of none other than Cade, carrying a little girl that looked no more than five years old or so, when the news source informed its readers that she was actually seven. It could have been the clash of sizes between man and child, or the fact he looked so powerful while she seemed ready to shatter at any given moment because of how thin and sickly frail she appeared, but my heart swelled despite old memories making their way to the forefront of my mind.

"Holy shit!" I breathed, my heart beating out of my chest.

Renegade's head popped up from his latest cuddle session with Molly and I looked over at the canine duo. He left his mistress and came to my side, nuzzling the hand nearest him that I had dropped onto the cushion next to me.

I turned to Renegade as the dog whined, pushing his head under my hand and began to run my fingers lightly through his fur, reading the article aloud.

Once done, I peered at the image before me again.

Cade was different from all others of his kind. He carried himself the same way his father used to when I'd known the man in my childhood. Beyond Cade and the newly rescued little girl, I noticed others trying to help the hero, but the look of determination on his face—the depth of it in his eyes—had me knowing he didn't need, nor did he want, their help. He did it because he needed to be the one there saving that life.

Right then, I knew I could fall for a man like Caden Summers and that frightened me about as much as it invigorated and excited me.

A wet swipe of a tongue drew me out of my musings to look once more at the German shepherd before me.

"Bet you could have found her faster than our man Cade, huh?" I ruffled the top of his head with an upward tick of my lips.

Renegade barked his agreement, or what I assumed it to be just that, making me laugh.

. . .

It wasn't until the second day Cade was away, following a lengthy hike through the woods with both Renegade and Molly, that I began to feel unsettled. I couldn't quite put my finger on it, but things were looking different inside my little haven of a cottage. Minuscule differences really, but enough to make me feel on edge.

Now, if I were being honest with myself, the eerie feeling of being watched over the last month which had only grown should have been the first inkling things weren't as peaceful as they once were. I'd been in my head so much that I'd brushed it off, thinking my absentmindedness was the culprit to me putting things out of their regular places—like my missing book.

Sure, it had been the first of many little discrepancies, but it was far from the last one, the frequency with which things disappeared or were moved were becoming alarming.

Once I'd gotten back from Cade's house yesterday, I'd taken the time to look at my shelves to ensure I hadn't simply misplaced the copy I'd accused the man of keeping for himself. Hell, I'd even looked in the most unusual of places, thinking that I'd been so distracted as of late, perhaps I'd stashed the paperback somewhere like the freezer, or inside a bathroom drawer or some other nonsense, even though it wasn't like me to do that, no matter how preoccupied I could get.

I never found it.

Staring at my cottage, Renegade seemed to pick up on the fact something wasn't quite right. I couldn't pinpoint it though. Then Molly began to bark just as her mate moved ahead of both of us females and took a defensive stance and released the most ferocious growl I'd ever witnessed. Chills raced down my spine.

"Cut it out, you two," I ordered, as I approached the side of my cottage where I kept a locked rifle in my shed. Yes, I was so unsettled that I suddenly felt the need to arm myself with more than two dogs who'd by then were simmering at a growl, their attention solely on my front door.

As I climbed the steps, I was thankful I had a small key ring. Careful of minimizing the amount of noise, I slipped the key in and turned, holding tight enough so the deadbolt didn't make its usual snick-and-click noise.

Turning the knob, the creak I'd gotten so accustomed to over the years—and evidently forgot about—made itself heard; loud enough for any intruder to get the one-up on me.

And that's when I heard it.

Both dogs barreled past me, nearly knocking me on my ass, and ran into my bedroom, barking, snarling, slobbering messes just as a loud bang graced my ears.

I hurried into my room, rifle at the ready, to find personal items strewn everywhere. My bedroom window was left open, my curtains swaying out the sill in the gentle breeze. There was no sign of an intruder, who clearly had escaped the wrath of my two protective canines and the heat I was packing.

Lowering my weapon, I rushed to the window and peered out, knowing all too well whoever it had been was now long gone. My safe haven was no longer as such.

thirteen

ASPEN

AS I TIDIED up the mess in my cottage, taking pictures of the scene with my phone to document things, the dogs had only begun to calm down. Renegade had pretty much stood sentry over me, watching every move I made. Molly, the loyal pooch she was, had been at his side, but there was no disputing who was the alpha between the two dogs.

My emotions were riding high, and every little snap of a tree branch, an acorn hitting the cottage's roof, or loud rustling of leaves seemed to have me on edge. My surroundings no longer felt as peaceful as they would seem to any outsider.

I was unsettled—freaked the hell out to be honest.

My privacy had been invaded—*violated*.

I was used to being by myself, my seclusion from the world was perceived as an equivalent to safety for me. Now, my remoteness felt more like my personal prison. I had no idea who my intruder was, what they wanted, or if they'd be back. That last fact terrified me shitless, but I refused to run. I would stand my ground. And if things escalated, I'd call the cops.

As a coping mechanism to any form of stress or anxiety, I had always been one to gravitate toward cleaning, which is why I was still hard at it nearly three hours later.

My bedroom now smelled of lemon and pine, and I swear I could see my own reflection in the hardwood floors. Hell, I was shocked the finish on said surface still existed, with the amount of scrubbing I had subjected it to. My level of cleanliness at the moment truly rivaled that of any hospital or top-notch medical facility. I'd even washed the walls, the furniture, and bed linens.

Okay, so I went a little overboard, but you too would be just a little crazy when your sanctuary, your favorite place in the whole world, had been sullied by being invaded by some mere stranger with who knows what kind of an agenda.

It wasn't until I was storing my various cleaning products under the kitchen sink that I turned and noticed the state of my library. Being that every piece of literature held a sacred place in my heart, panic swelled when I saw those titles in complete disarray. To any onlooker, it would appear like the ever-perfect prolific title listing of a rabid reader, but I was particular when I acquired a new piece for my collection, and what I was staring at right then was far from the way I displayed my preciouses.

Even the dogs noticed my state of unrest. Molly approached me to nudge my hand, as she often did when I felt troubled or stressed.

"We'll fix it, girl." I patted her head, the feel of her fur sifting through my fingers calming me. Then I turned for my desk, grabbed my laptop, thankful it had a sturdy case, which had saved it from being destroyed after being flung—something I presumed my interloper had done as I'd found it on the floor across the room—and pulled the database of titles I owned that I'd built what felt like ages ago. With my arsenal in hand, I proceeded to right the wrongs, my senses calming with every bit of progress I made.

By dinnertime, I collapsed on the couch, a fire roaring in the hearth with a grilled cheese sandwich and a glass of pinot grigio at the ready. Molly and Renegade were snuggled by the soothing flames and the easy-listening words of the *Rat Pack* sufficed to chase away the remnants of the day's restlessness and tension.

CADE

I'd caught the shadow in my periphery long before my truck came to a full stop, the hairs rising on the back of my neck. Slamming on the brakes, the tires slid across the gravel drive, and I hurried out, no thought of a flashlight, my phone the only thing that could be of help with its built-in flashlight app.

I could hear barking and snarling, but by the time I reached the edge of the forest, whatever I thought I'd seen was long gone. And so, I waited...listened, but nothing came, and my sense of unease didn't dissipate, even when the barks turned to whines.

Approaching the porch steps, the whining grew louder. As I turned the knob and pushed inward, I was rewarded with an immovable barrier.

"Aspen?" I called out above the pathetic doggy noises and scraping at the door.

"Cade?"

My body stiffened as I heard the distinctive sound of metal and wood clunk down onto the floor. Something was up and my gut was screaming at me that once I got behind the tiny cottage's front door, I wouldn't like what I found.

The instant the front door swooped inward I was tackled by a crazed Amazon, who propelled me back two steps in order to keep us from tumbling on the ground.

Molly and Renegade circled around us, barking before taking off as if on the hunt for what I presumed was the shadow figure I had spotted upon my arrival.

Looking over Aspen's shoulder, I saw a rifle haphazardly lying on the living room floor and focused on the wreck of a beauty in my arms. "Pen?" I hurried us in and bolted the door behind us. "What's going on?"

"I—I thought," she swallowed, trying to regain her composure, "you were someone else."

My brows pinched low in confusion and my body became one solid mass. "Explain. Now."

fourteen

BY THE TIME Aspen finished her tale about finding her place in complete disarray and that whoever had been inside had escaped through her bedroom window, my concern for her safety had grown exponentially.

Needless to say, my suspicion the shadow figure I'd spotted on arrival was of the human and not animal variety had me worried about our dogs who were still running amok outside.

"We need to find Molly," Aspen said.

"Renegade won't let anything happen to her," I stated, as sure as my words sounded, "but you're both coming home with me."

"What? No!"

"Until we have this figured out, you're not staying here alone, and since I have to give a SITREP to Dalton about this last case, I can't stay here with you tonight," I explained.

"I'm not going to give this asshole all of the power," she argued.

"That's not for debate, sweetheart." My eyes bored into

92

hers, pleading she'd give me just a small reprieve. Tomorrow would be another day to reevaluate things and figure where we would go from there.

"Fine." She crossed her arms over her chest. "For tonight."

Thank fuck!

"Good. Now that we have that settled, let's go find the mutts, pack some clothes for you, and get out of here."

And that's what we did.

ASPEN

Okay, so I was annoyed as all get out with the way Cade seemed to have swooped in and rescued me from my stressful predicament, but I'd be lying if I didn't preface that with the fact his utter alpha bossiness had also been a sexy-as-hell trait. For the first time since I'd been younger, someone had taken charge of things and allowed me the luxury of feeling my emotions instead of fighting them for self-preservation purposes. It was a foreign concept for me, but not an unwelcome one.

As I sipped my peppermint tea, peering at an otherwise dark backyard that overlooked another dense copse of trees from the large picture window, illuminated by the sliver of moon peeking out from the occasional cloud in the starry night sky, I pondered the facts as I knew them, and wondered what my options would be at this very point in time.

"Those must be some heavy thoughts," Cade muttered, as his arms came around me and tugged me back into the warmth of his chest before kissing the side of my hair. His breath stirred goosebumps over my flesh.

"Mm—hmm."

"Penny for your thoughts?"

The saying had me giggling silently as I turned to catch

sight of the scruff on his chin, unable to turn my body to face him completely with the lock he had around me. "Seriously?" I smiled.

He chuckled. "My mom used to ask that question when she suspected my dad or I had something weighing heavily on our minds," he said by way of explaining.

"Just thinking about what I can do," I told him. "I could go to the police, but who's going to post a unit that far into the woods? Chances are, whoever it was would just move on if they saw a cruiser parked out there on the regular. What I can't seem to wrap my head around is this person's motive. That's what bothers me most."

"The world is filled with freaks," he said.

A singular eyebrow arched at his words. "Yeah, but in the bush?"

"You'd be surprised, and with what you've been through as a kid, you would know better than anybody what kind of degenerates lurk in the oddest of places."

That had me pulling away from him, anger bubbling up. "Why the fuck would you say that?" The appeal and calming effect of my tea was all but gone and my body had grown cold at his words. The look of regret strewn across his face did little to assuage the frustration I felt.

"I'm sorry," Cade said, "but it's not like we can forget what happened to Willow." He ran his hand through his hair and down his face before shaking his head. "Forget I brought it up."

The loss of my sister was something I'd never get past. Hell, he felt his own variation of loss with regards to my own experience, seeing as his father had been deeply linked with the investigation. Christ, he'd lost his father in part because of my sister's case.

Before I could say something I'd regret, I turned toward Cade's kitchen and marched to dump the rest of my drink in the sink before reaching for the dishwasher to stow my soiled cup.

I was startled by the man of the house grabbing my arm gently. "Pen...please." He turned me toward him, the worry he'd really screwed things up so palpable that my anger dissipated some.

I sighed. "It wasn't fair of you to bring that up," I said, even though I knew he didn't mean it in a malicious way.

"I'm sorry," he repeated, but I couldn't quite meet his gaze until his hand lightly forced my chin upward. "I'm just worried about you."

My eyes searched his right then.

"I want to make sure you're safe." He sighed, shaking his head as though trying to figure out how best to proceed next. "Hell, if I thought you'd be in agreement, I'd pack your shit and move you in here until we figured this situation out, but I know that shit isn't going to fly with you and we're not at that stage of our relationship yet."

Relationship?

We didn't really have one, but I'd be dishonest with him—with myself—if I denied that emotions and attraction were guiding us in that exact direction. Just a few mornings ago, had the time permitted it, I'd have had him cradled between my naked thighs, reveling in the power he exuded over my body. Oh, the pleasure he could bring a lonely spinster like myself!

"I respect you too much to stifle and strong-arm you into making you do my bidding," his eyes glittered with the sincerity of his words. "It's so far from the reason why I'm attracted to you." My heart fluttered. "Your independence, that fire you've got, it's all part of what draws me in." He kissed my forehead, then lifted his head, his arms pulling me toward him, settling on my waist. "And as much as I hate the idea of you alone out there, and maybe it's the fact that today has shaken you, babe, but I can't let go of the feeling in my gut that tells me whatever is going on with this fucker isn't quite done yet."

My hands lifted to land on his chest as I relaxed into Cade's hold. "Can we look into a security system?" I blurted out.

Cade's eyes widened in surprise, and the warmth in his smile and his gaze told me he was definitely supportive of the idea.

"First thing tomorrow," he assured me. "And we'll log a report too. I want you to come with me into Nightshade and talk to the guys about what's going on."

"Cade," I started, but the man shut me up with a quick peck.

"We're not going to the cops. Not right now. The guys and I can handle this, and you're right...whoever this is will fuck off if they know they're being watched. I want whoever this is to be caught," he explained, "and part of that is us catching him in the middle of whatever act he's got coming next. It also gives us something to give to the police when the time is right, if we ever get to that point."

As insensitive as this conversation had started, Cade sure knew how to redeem himself in the way of painting a picture of why his thoughts had initially led him to say what he had that set me off. The man cared and if I'd let him, he'd help me grow into myself, giving my life a new and increasingly beautiful meaning.

"Kiss me," I whispered.

And he didn't disappoint.

fifteen

CADE

THE INSTANT ASPEN'S eyes softened, then proceeded to dilate, I knew I'd redeemed myself from the stupidity I'd blurted out without a thought to her sensitivities. I was such a tool sometimes when it meant sharing my emotions; but when I broke that barrier and got started, the words would spew out of me like a bad bout of verbal diarrhea. And they had.

The minute my mouth met Aspen's, I knew tonight would be *it*.

Our initial reunion from my latest case had been a less-than-desirable event, but it had led us to this very moment, and I was going to take everything the woman in my arms was willing to give me.

Aspen eagerly licked at my lips, and I opened to allow her entrance, understanding what had happened earlier had culminated in a sense of loss of control, one I wanted her to reclaim. I groaned as she took possession, but all bets were off the moment she sucked my tongue into her mouth. There was only so much I could take.

In an abrupt move, I grabbed Aspen under her arms and twisted us to drop her to sit on the island countertop. Roughly pushing her thighs apart with my body, I wedged myself against her core, my hands grabbing on to her head, tangling into her hair. I took her mouth, devouring her, hopefully conveying the urgency of my hunger for her.

"Cade..." The need flooding her voice had me burning hotter as my lips began a delicious trail down her neck, the flavor of her skin urging me to discover what the rest of her tasted like.

"Pen..." My hands wandered down her back, holding her closer than close, firmly continuing their downward trajectory to her ass to pull her against my swollen cock, grinding myself into her, cursing the layers of clothes that prevented me from feeling her skin against mine.

"Take me to bed, Cade," she begged, as I nipped her collarbone.

Her permission had me drawing back enough to gaze into her eyes. "You're sure?"

The smile that spread across her face was one I'd only seen directed toward her laptop screen: that conniving and sexy little smirk. "Never been surer of anything in my life, other than when I made the decision to pursue publishing."

Well, fuck me!

"Hold on." I swear her eagerness had her moving to do just what I'd asked of her before the words were done pouring out of my mouth.

Aspen

There's nothing sexier than the partner I was involved with taking control of the situation and the sheer display of masculinity in their physical strength. I wasn't some spritely little slip of a thing and having Cade hold me in his arms with such effortlessness was the hottest thing I'd ever experienced. The way he wielded his body made me feel safe, cherished, and feminine; something I never thought I'd experience; both because of my size as well as the fact I was such a recluse.

He lightly deposited me on his bed, his body following to the mattress, covering mine as though he aimed to shelter me from some invisible storm. His lips gentled over my mouth, savoring me. Cade's eagerness showed in his restraint, his tremoring muscles a dead giveaway to his growing hunger. The affect I held over this man was empowering to witness at such close proximity.

I was the first to reach for an item of clothing, shoving my hands down his back and under his shirt—fisting the bottom of it—and shimmying it up to his shoulders as he distracted himself with the top of my cleavage, the access given by how my shirt had stretched low due to the friction of our bodies.

The moment Cade pulled away to help get rid of his shirt as he straddled my hips, the urge to feel the firmness of his chest against the naked flesh of my tits became all-consuming. As he chucked the T-shirt off to the side, I did some half-assed crunch and peeled my own light sweater over my head, then reached for the back clasp of my bra.

I'd never been this brazen with a partner before, but the heat in Cade's gaze—the way his body reacted to mine—had me wanting to bare myself to him, giving him back what he'd been giving me without knowing.

"Beautiful," he whispered, his gaze skimming my chest and I swear I could feel it daintily scalding my skin like the softest of caresses.

"Yes..." I barely recognized my voice as I reached out a single hand, physically having to touch the Adonis before me. "You are." A single finger tickled the soft, barely-there treasure trail that peeked over his low-slung jeans, sneaking under the edge of the material, gingerly rubbing the back of the digit against the warm skin hidden behind as our eyes connected.

His breath hitched, then his hands hurried to relieve some pressure by popping the button and unzipping his fly before he proceeded to fan the flames.

Grabbing my wandering hand, then reaching for the other, his fingers intertwined with mine as he raised them up by my head, pressing them into the mattress, all the while his eyes begging permission.

"Leave them there," he rasped, once he realized I wasn't going to fight him.

My mouth ran dry, rendering me speechless, so I nodded my response.

Backing away slightly, he let his fingers skim my inner arms, pausing to tickle the inside of my elbows, while his eyes followed his hand's movements. Caressing my shoulders, a singular digit traced my collarbones before trailing lower to my breasts, my nipples pebbling at the sensation. I craved more.

The moment Cade's warm wet tongue flicked one nipple and a hand pinched at the other, my back arched into him, demanding he continue.

"Delicious," he managed before licking a path to my other breast, circling my other nipple with his tongue prior to sucking it into his mouth, inflicting the same treatment he had to the first. He moved the one free hand, that wasn't propping him over me, down to my core and cupped my heat. Growling, he raised his eyes to mine. "I can't wait to taste your pussy." My hips flexed, searching for the pressure I needed to get me closer to release. "I'm willing to bet you taste best, right here." His middle finger rubbed hard against my slit, the friction of material against my damp folds feeling amazing.

"Yes," I panted.

In the quickest instant, Cade's weight disappeared, and his calloused hands were yanking my yoga pants down my hips, along with my underwear, then he was right *there*!

"Cade!" I squealed, as he pushed his nose into the top of my folds, taking a huge inhalation of my scent.

"Fuck," he groaned as a finger gingerly traced my slickened slit. "So fucking hot." A lick from bottom to top had me whimpering. "So fucking wet." His thumb flicked my clit, causing a full-body shudder to quake through me, then my arms moved down to my sides, fisting the sheets. "I'm going to eat you up so good, baby."

"Mm—hmm-ungh," was my response since my world had begun to spin on a new axis.

CADE

I've always enjoyed eating a woman out, but that first taste of Aspen's essence had me on the verge of bursting in my pants. Her smell, the sweet tang of her juices, the way she responded to the minimal touch of my ministrations had me fighting the urge to skip all of the good stuff and get to the great, by shoving my dick inside her so deep. I'd make it so it would take us over the edge so hard and fast that neither of us would be able to tell what was up or down; scramble our brains so much, ultimately leaving us sated with the urge to start over on an endless loop.

As much as I wanted to get to the grand finale, it wasn't the kind of lover I prided myself to be; it wasn't right for any time in my book, but it sure as shit wasn't right for my first time with Aspen.

My questing finger delved deeper, testing her readiness as I licked up one side of her pussy lips, down to the other.

"More!" she pleaded.

"More *what*?" I smirked up at her. Her fiery hair was spread wildly over my pillows, her head was arched back sexily, exposing her slim neck, eyes closed. "Look at me, Pen." Her gaze snapped down to meet mine. "Tell me." I pulled my finger out, joining a second into her heat, curving it upward until I felt the ribbed swollen tissue and made a light tapping motion before withdrawing. "Tell me what you need and I'll give you everything."

"That!"

"*What*, Aspen?" I repeated my double-digit penetration and subtle tapping, feeling her pussy flutter against my fingers, trying to keep me inside her as I pulled out once more. "This?" I added a long lick up her glistening lips, sucking lightly on her clit, grazing it gently with my teeth before blowing over the swollen nub.

"Yes!" she panted. "All of it. Please, please, please! Make me come." Her eyes pleaded in total desperation. "Make me come in your mouth. I want to kiss you and taste myself."

Holy shit!

This woman was the biggest wet dream come to life and as much as I liked the idea of giving her a little edging anticipation, I suddenly needed to see her unravel before my eyes as much as I wanted to shoot my load in her depths, flooding her with my cum. And when we were done, I'd then taste the mixture of us when we were both ready to go again by getting her to fall over the precipice with my mouth once more.

So, I hit that pussy hard, sucking her clit like a beast as I inserted two digits into her heat, going to town on that spongy bit of nerves I knew would send her into the stratosphere. She braced her feet on the mattress, further opening herself up to me. Her hips flexed into my face, spreading her juices into the scruff surrounding my mouth just as her hands snagged my head, pulling me against her.

She was so close, and with a singular command, she detonated for me.

ASPEN

Because Cade had me so amped up, I never thought twice about flinching out of embarrassment when his agile fingers pulled from me, soaked to his forearms and dripping as he licked and sucked them. The look of utter pleasure and satisfaction beaming from his ruggedly handsome face, the fact the entire bottom of his face glistened with my wetness, only made me want to lick him all over with urgency. My thighs were still quaking from the strength of my orgasm, the sheets beneath my ass were soaked and I found myself limp yet still famished for more somehow.

What this man did to me. God!

Cade slowly backed away to stand beside the bed, his eyes never leaving mine. With warmth filling me at the heat in his gaze, it kept me focused on him—us—my body at a new level of boiling instead of feeling cold and bereft.

The man pushed his jeans down his hips, kicking the lot, including his underwear and socks, then turned to his dresser, retracting a box of condoms, and pulling a strip of rubbers from it while I gloried in the perfection that was his firmly chiseled ass.

I wonder how he'd react if I took a bite out of that thing? Where delectable derrieres were concerned, Albert Caden Summers won over any of my former partners, the various heroes in my books, and the cover models I've worked with in the past. Hands. Down.

I jumped out of my lust-filled daze when I felt the man of my latest obsessions push my legs farther apart as he crawled nearer. His hands smoothed up my body while his lips followed close behind, bringing me back up to a low simmer.

The moment his face was close enough to grab on to, I pulled his mouth up to mine, the subtle scent of my essence causing a flutter in my stomach and saliva to pool in my mouth. I took his lips in a ravenous kiss, plunging my tongue into his mouth to take what I needed.

"You taste fucking amazing, baby." He groaned as he pushed his naked cock against my folds and flexed his hips, slickening things with the by-product of my previous orgasm. "I can't fucking wait to be inside you; to feel you clamping around my dick, strangling it with that tight pussy of yours."

"Do it," I urged him. "I need to feel you inside me."

He didn't waste any time. Before I knew it, he'd grabbed the condom packet off the sheets next to my hip, made quick work of things, and was suited up.

Guiding my legs over his shoulders, he reached out for one of the pillows I wasn't resting on, tapped my hip without words so I could lift, and shoved it under my ass.

With no preamble, he guided himself to my entrance, pushing in so the very tip of him was inside me.

"Oh God!" came out breathlessly.

"So perfect," he gritted out between clenched teeth, pushing in a bit farther, then pausing once more. "Perfect for me." His eyes snagged mine as he eased in until his balls were pressed against my ass.

"Yes..." The word was dragged out as I savored the slightly painful stretching sensation of my pussy around his length. The fullness. Those thoughts had me clenching on his girth, eliciting a hiss from him.

"Fuck, babe, I'm not gonna last if you keep doing that." His hips pulled back as his hands soothed downward until he settled them at the junction of my thighs, a thumb coming to circle my swollen clit, causing me to twitch. "Ah yeah. Fuck!" he said, sounding marveled at the feel of us coming together.

"So good," I muttered, my hands lifting to land on his abs, rubbing up his stomach to stop and tweak his hardened nipples.

"Baby..." he groaned, his eyes closing with enjoyment at my ministrations.

The combination of my light pinches and the flexing of my Kegels had Cade breaking.

"Fuck. Shit." The expression in his eyes looked almost pained. He dropped my legs so the backs of my knees rested on his forearms and he leaned closer over me, thus spreading me even more open. "Hold on, baby. This is going to be fast."

And he didn't lie.

sixteen

ASPEN

PAIN.

Sweet pain. Okay, so it was more of an ache—a rather deli-cious one at that—as I stretched out for the first time upon waking.

Well-used. That's how I could sum up how last night had gone down with Cade.

The man was a sex god! He could pull off any of the follow-ing: the sultry and sweet, the downright dirty, and the vanilla.

My mind flitted to the part of the night before, when he had mentioned the addition of toys, spanking, and light bites of pain to more future sexual forays, causing my body to warm with need. The mere thought of it all now had me wriggling as I squeezed my legs together.

Cade's arms around me tightened.

"Good morning." He kissed the back of my head, then nuzzled into my neck, scraping his teeth against the tendon ran down to meet my shoulder and I felt myself moisten. The tingling in my nether regions caused me to press my ass snugger to Cade's hardening cock. His devious chuckle shook the entire bed and had me creaming myself further. "Hungry?" he asked.

I reached behind my ass, giving myself enough room to grab on to his length and squeezed it until he hissed. "Famished." I smirked, turned in his arms to face him, then nipped at his chin, urging him to his back. Proceeding to shimmy down his body, my lips and hands tortured him in a similar way he had done to me the previous night.

Pushing the blankets down to the bottom of the bed, I coaxed Cade's legs apart with my knees, making room for myself between them.

"This is by far the best buffet I've ever had," I said, as I lowered my head to lick the indentation of the deep 'V' at his pelvis, nudging the tip of his cock out of the way with my chin.

"Really," he husked.

With no warning, I opened my mouth and slid my lips and tongue over his length, lowering until I nearly gagged, then pulled back until only the head of his cock remained in my mouth.

"Mm-hmm," I hummed.

Cade's eyes widened. "Jesus, woman!"

I released him, licking the tip of him and the accumulating precum there, as if he were the best tasting lollipop, before pulling back enough to grin up at him, then I got back to work.

"Dammit, Pen..." he groaned, as I plunged down on him once more, trailing a hand to play with his balls. "You'll be the death of me," he finished as I sucked him deeper, attempting something I'd never felt eager enough to try before. "Oh, fuck!"

CADE

The moment my cock nudged the back of her throat, my mouth ran dry as she swallowed. I've always been a fan of the mutual giving of head, but never had I had a woman able to take me down her throat like Aspen was doing right then.

Her eyes watered, saliva leaked out the sides of her mouth, but my grunts and groans only seemed to spur her on. So much so she straddled my leg and began rubbing her dripping pussy in such a way that her endgame would have both of us satisfied, as well as leaving me with an added excuse to have her coming on my cock again before we had to head out for our meeting with Dalton and the rest of the crew on shift at NSI.

The instant my balls drew up, I gasped out, "Baby, I'm gonna come. If you don't want me blowing in that sinful mouth of yours, you better—"

She didn't give me the chance to finish, because she pulled back, grabbed my hand, laced our fingers together, then directed them to the back of her head, tangling our digits in her tresses. Plunging her mouth down, her suction seemed to double in intensity before swallowing once more.

I was done.

She killed me, but what a fucking way to go!

I swear she'd sucked my brains straight down my body and out through my dick.

By the time the fog of bliss cleared from my mind, our entwined hands were still where Aspen had brought them, and she was delicately nuzzling my cock, her head resting against my thigh, her breathing heavy, and eyes glazed over.

"Get up here, baby," I whispered to her, releasing her hand, then threading my fingers in her hair in such a way I could fist it without causing her any pain. I tilted her head up so I could see her entire face.

She was wobbly in her movements, so as soon as she was close enough for me to grab on to, I pulled her the rest of the way up, settling her so she was draped over my body, her head resting on my chest while we both finished coming back down to Earth.

By the time we reached Nightshade's headquarters, it was nearing lunch and therefore Aspen and I had picked the guys up an assortment of sandwiches, soft drinks, and potato chips after calling beforehand for a head count.

"'Bout fucking time you showed up," Brycen approached hurriedly, grabbed our bags, and ran off to the back of the office suite where the small eat-in kitchen was. Rex, Dalton, and his wife, Devolin, were hot on his heels.

"Vultures," I blurted, laughing at Aspen's humored expression. "All of them," I mumbled as kissed her temple.

"It is one thirty," she responded, then her body stiffened, her gaze her gaze having trailed from me, had set itself on someone else and widened.

When I turned to see what had captured her attention, Devolin had returned to us, and was standing in front of my woman, eyeing her from head to toe. "You're not at all what I'd pictured you to be," she said. "Rex told me who you were back there. Please tell me he wasn't yanking my chain. You...you're Penny Sexton, right?"

The woman at my side proffered her hand and said, "Aspen Ridge. The photo on the back of those books isn't the real me. It's the corporate world exerting their rights to dictate things."

Devolin snorted at the formal kind of greeting, grabbed Aspen's hand, and then her into a tight hug. "I'm Devolin. It's such a pleasure meeting the woman who's gotten this big lug to smile so much over the last month," she stated, then promptly released her, and reached out to hold both Aspen's hands. "And those books of yours...*hot!*"

The blush that suffused Aspen's face was the first indication my companion felt slightly uncomfortable from the attention and praise.

"Um...thanks," she muttered.

"You're welcome," Devolin said, then backed away. "I'm sorry I came right at you, but I've been reading you since you started and when the guys told me they knew you, I got a little over-excited."

Aspen simply shrugged, then bit her bottom lip, and I knew her mind had wandered off momentarily. Then her face lit up with recognition. "Devolin...the hacker, right?" She looked over at me with a twinkle in her eyes. I nodded in response and when we both turned to face Dalton's wife, her eyes held wonder as if she'd scored the biggest prize—being recognized by who she'd deemed a celebrity.

Devolin's eyes rounded. "You've heard of me?" she asked.

Aspen nodded. "I've been meaning to call you up," she said. "Dalton gave me your card. I wanted to pick your brain about a character I'm developing. I was wondering—"

"Yes!" Devolin jumped up and down excitedly. "Wait until Emberlyn hears about this."

"Ember is our friend Shane's wife," I explained, wrapping my arm around Aspen's shoulders and tugging her into my side. "Shane's a detective with the Jacksonville police department. He also works with us here part time, kind of like me, the only difference is he's looking to shirk his day-job to focus on his new wife, their family, and assuming his part-ownership of this place." She nodded in understanding despite looking slightly overwhelmed with the wealth of information I'd just spewed at her.

"Come on," Devolin said. "Let's go get some lunch before Babyface eats our portion."

I laughed at her hurried expression, but I couldn't blame her. If given the chance, he probably would.

ASPEN

"Still to this day, I can't believe I told him he could put me in handcuffs and have his wicked way with me," Devolin giggled, unaware her husband Dalton's gaze held a mixture of heat and adoration pointed in his wife's direction as she prattled on. Every now and again, she'd reach for his hand to give it a squeeze while he was seated, straddling the side of her chair, much like Cade had done to mine.

Suffice to say, as soon as we had joined Devolin's husband and the rest of the NSI team on shift, I found myself feeling immediately at ease despite the exponential level of testosterone in the smallish room. Even with her initial aggressive approach, I found I liked Devolin almost immediately. Kindred spirits and all, seeing as she wasn't much for getting out either, due in part to her living with severe medical issues most of her life.

"Aspen, Cade mentioned you'd had an uninvited guest yesterday?" Dalton broke the jovial feel of the early afternoon.

I nearly choked myself to death on the final sip of my soda, causing a ruckus of a cough and sputtering. My only response was in the form of an animated nod, while I attempted to dab at my eyes, which had filled with tears, with a napkin. My throat was on fire, and Cade seemed to pick up on it as he rushed to the sink and filled a glass of water, bringing it over, and wrapping my hand around it.

"Drink."

After a few minutes, I regained my breath and was able to continue the conversation.

"Yeah," I rasped and took a nervous sip before continuing. "I was out for a morning hike with the dogs. Nothing seemed weirder than normal while we were out."

"What do you mean by that?" Dalton leaned forward. His undivided attention was pointed solely at me. I felt the tension ratchet up around me, causing me to look around, noticing every man's attention—Rex, Brycen and Cade—was focused solely in my direction.

"I thought it was me, that I've been off my game... I've been distracted lately, but things have been weird at home for the last month or so," I told them. "They're just subtle things though, like my keys not always being where I would leave them, or crumbs on the counter when I always clean up after making food. Things like that."

"The book," Cade added to which I nodded. "It's escalating, Pen." Then he whispered the next so no one could hear, "I have to say, I'm a little pissed you haven't shared this with me, baby. When we get home, we're going to have a chat about why you haven't said anything until now."

I turned my head to look at him, brows furrowed. "But you knew—"

"Don't you finish that sentence, sweetheart." He grabbed my chin to keep our gazes connected. "We can't help you unless you tell us everything. The smallest detail can mean so much in the grander scheme of things." Then, his other hand sifted into my hair, pulled my face to his, and he gently nibbled my bottom lip before sealing his lips to mine in a gesture that soothed my nerves as much as it seemed to do the same for him, if the look in his eyes was anything to go by once he'd pulled away.

"I'm sorry," I whispered.

He nodded, but never said anything else as he turned toward the rest of the room, a devilish smirk strewn across his mouth. The guys each sported a look of humor on theirs, and questions in their eyes, while Devolin giggled away before mouthing, "Hot" my way, causing my lips to lift slightly at the edges before I caught myself.

Bugger! Cade had me wrapped around his little finger and he didn't even know it. Or maybe he did.

seventeen

BY THREE THAT AFTERNOON, Cade and I were back at my tiny cottage with both dogs, waiting for some guy named Stan to show up.

According to the guys at Nightshade, Stan was the best there was for any level of security system you could imagine. With that, and the fact I had committed a faux pas in Cade's eyes with not having divulged everything until today, I heeded his and the men's wishes by employing Safe & SEALed to provide me with the security I needed.

At four, Stan was knocking at my front door.

"Stay," Cade commanded as he hurried ahead of me to answer.

I pouted, crossing my arms over my chest, and let myself drop onto the sofa. "It's Stan, Cade."

"You don't know him. I do. And even though he's expected, it could be someone entirely different out there." He looked through the window next to the front door, nodded, then proceeded to unlatch the deadbolt and pulled the door inward.

"Cade," the man I had yet to see said. A proffered hand clasped Cade's and the two shook.

"Stan, good to see you. Thanks for making it on such short notice." Cade cleared the door and allowed the other man entry.

"It's no problem," he said, then trained his eyes in my direction.

Before me stood a mountain of a man, hair cut military precision short, tattoo sleeves beautifully adorning his arms, or what I could see of them where his tightly fitted polo shirt wasn't covering.

"You must be Aspen." Stan smiled the softest of smiles that contrasted with his size—which screamed *killer* by the way—and stuck out his hand. "I knew when Cade called, another woman was in trouble before he even said anything."

My brow arched with my confusion, but nonetheless, I put my much smaller hand in his, letting his gentle grip swallow it whole. "It's nice to meet you, Stan."

The man held on to me a little longer than I deemed comfortable, his gaze studying me, penetrating as if he could read my thoughts, my emotions. He learned me without words. And it had me feeling twitchy.

As Cade came to stand at our sides, Stan's gaze broke from mine and turned to him. "I like her." Stan dropped my hand, then proceeded to walk toward the back of the cottage, also known as my bedroom. "I'll start here," he said over his shoulder.

Before I knew it, Stan and Cade had decided my cottage would be outfitted with sensor lights, window, door and interior sensors—I was assured Molly wouldn't be able to set them off in the dead of the night without my asking—cameras, and a control panel. It didn't matter that I was the homeowner; the men had taken free rein on my safety, and according to Cade, money was no object.

. . .

CADE

I could tell she was pissed at me, just by the way the door had latched loudly behind Stan after she'd given him a charming thanks. Then, she turned the deadbolt to the lock position with a little more force than necessary. Without those aforementioned tells, the fact she now stood ramrod straight, her shoulders bunched up to her ears, along with her breathing having picked up, those served as great indicators to her current mood.

Resigned—and a little turned on to witness such fire directed at me—I sat down on the couch and settled in. "Say it."

A snort. "Say what?"

"What you're thinking. Feeling." I sighed. "I know you've got your panties in a bunch about something, Pen, so why don't you just tell me what it is I did that's got you so worked up."

She spun to face me with a look of incredulity. "You mean, you don't know?"

"Of course, I don't," I told her. "I wouldn't have asked if I did, sweetheart."

"Ha!" Her gaze strayed to just beside my face. She was unable to look me in the eye. "Funny, considering less than an hour ago you and Stan seemed to know what I needed without me saying a thing."

I couldn't help but smirk at that. "Baby," I cajoled, getting to my feet as Aspen chose to back away from my advances, her hands making a motion to stave me off.

"Stop."

"Not gonna happen, Pen," I rasped, understanding where she was coming from now that I knew what was bothering her. My feet moved at a quick pace, backing her up against her front door, effectively barricading her in between my arms. "I'm not going to apologize for protecting what's mine, baby. You can bitch, scream, hit me if you will, but I'm not going to feel one ounce of guilt for protecting you."

Aspen's eyes had grown wide, and she was biting her lower lip.

I smirked. "Nothing to say, sweetheart?"

Her mouth dropped open, but no words came. When she realized her speechless state, she snapped it shut, then growled before her chin met her chest in a gesture of capitulation.

I couldn't help myself. I reached to grab her chin, tilting her head back so I could see her eyes. "I know you're a grown woman who can make her damn mind up about her own safety. I know Stan and I went a little over the top, but—"

And there was that spark again. "A little?" she mumbled, as my thumb reached her bottom lip, giving it a gentle back and forth rub.

I nodded. "I just found you and if this is going where I think it is, I'm not taking any chances."

There. My cards were all laid out on the proverbial table.

ASPEN

Okay, so I was still pissed at him.

And confused.

It had only been a month and a half really since we'd met. We'd spent a total of five days of that in each other's presence. So how was it that a reclusive woman, such as myself, had gone from not wanting to settle with a man to feeling like I didn't want to let this particular specimen standing before me go? The shift was recent—as recent as yesterday—if I was being honest with myself. An image of Cade carrying that little girl, the news video of him giving a death glare to anyone who tried to intercept his forward progress by removing the tiny burden from his arms. Yes, that was the moment things really changed for me. The fact that, since I'd known him, he'd been an all-or-nothing kind of man in everything he undertook should have been more than enough to convince me I was a goner, but I'd fought it. And lost.

You're done for, you idiot woman, you.

I was.

And the rubbing of his thumb on my lower lip right then? The man didn't need words to make me melt. With such a simple gesture, I was putty in his hands.

"Okay," I rasped, my mouth having gone dry.

His brows furrowed. "*Okay*?"

"Uh-huh." I licked my lips, my tongue brushing the tip of his thumb in the process, and his eyes darkened.

"Okay." His face grew nearer as he leaned in and paused. "Pen?"

My eyes grew heavy, and my body hummed. "Hmm?"

His lips quirked. "Mine," he growled, before he slammed his mouth down on mine, taking what he had just declared was his.

Mine, I thought as my mouth was otherwise occupied to say the word back to him, but I sure as hell showed him this thing between us was more than a one-way street.

eighteen

CADE

SOMETHING SHIFTED up against that front door of Aspen's cottage. The moment my lips met hers, I sensed it.

Reluctantly pulling away from the woman who was thoroughly flushed from my kisses, I pecked her lips once more and presented her with her options. "Here or home?"

"Here." She tightened her arms around my neck, pulling herself to her tiptoes, and rubbed herself against my front, eliciting a groan from me. "Right here, Mr. Summers." An arm dropped, and her hand tapped lightly against the wooden barrier to her home's main entrance.

Fuck me!

Closing my eyes, I took a deep breath in through my nose, then released it before peering down at her. "You'll be the death of me," I muttered and moved my hands down to her ass, squeezing it as a signal for her to jump up. "I'm not fucking you against this door...not yet anyway."

She beamed a smile at me. "Not yet?"

I shook my head and turned us toward the inner sanctuary of the cottage. "Ever since we met, when you mumbled something about you never expecting this would be the way you'd have a man in your bed here, all I've been able to think about is getting you naked and sullying your sheets."

She giggled. "Is that right?" Her head tilted back as I began nuzzling the side of her neck, all the while bringing us to her bedroom.

"Mm-hmm." Her grip tightened on me as I leaned forward to place her on her bed, following her down until I was pressed on top of her.

As soon as we were settled, Aspen's grip loosened, and her arms moved to hold the slats of her headboard above her head. The move thrust her chest deeper into mine, and I could feel her pebbled nipples through our clothes.

Her eyes held mischief and I found myself captivated by her playfulness as she breathlessly said, "Sully away then."

ASPEN

Quick. Hard. Dirty.

I might have written about it, but I sure as fuck had never experienced the real thing. Cade rode me hard and put me away wet, and that wasn't just a metaphor either. I'm pretty sure I soaked through more than my sheets with how many times the man made me come.

Six. Fucking. Times! All this before he took his own release. Despite last night—I honestly thought it had been a complete fluke—I thought men like mine only existed in romance novels. I mean, why the hell else would us authors write about these types of lovers if not to fulfill a certain need we weren't getting on the regular, right? Sure, I always believed there were exceptions to the rule out there, but me landing one of those...nuh-uh, not little ol' me. Never.

A set of teeth bit down lightly on the back of my shoulder as a soapy hand caressed and tweaked the nipple of my breast. "Where's your head at, baby?" he mumbled against my drenched skin.

"How you're just too good to be true," I blurted, turning to face him. His deep blue gaze penetrated mine as though demanding I explain further. In order to distract him from my avoidance, I grabbed the bar of soap and proceeded to lather up his chest, my eyes aimed wherever my hands went, but my mouth also chose to run away on me. "Sexy. Sweet. Sensational. Insatiable. Kind. Dedicated. Strong." Each area of his body I cleansed was punctuated with a singular word until I was done.

Finding myself on my knees, face-to-face with a rather impressive erection, Cade made his thoughts known before I could get him off—a little something just for him.

"Up and out," he ground out, leaning past me to turn the water off.

He escorted me out of the shower, taking his time with dabbing my body with a towel as he himself dripped water onto the bathmat beneath his feet. His tongue joined his ministrations, catching the droplets he hadn't yet dabbed at on my shoulder, then my collarbone, moving tantalizingly slowly down my chest.

Making quick work of rubbing his chest and legs off with the same towel he'd used on me, he let the terry cloth sheet fall limp to the floor, then guided me backward toward my bed. That's when I noticed he'd changed the sheets.

I smirked as we toppled to the mattress. "I was wondering what took you so long before you joined me."

He smiled. "You're welcome." His lips pressed against mine for an all too quick peck before he gathered the duvet which he'd folded back and pulled it over us before he drew me snug against him.

Chest to chest, thigh to thigh, I lay in Cade's arms, reveling in the heat of his skin against mine, captive in his affectionate gaze.

"Sleep," he whispered, kissing my forehead and giving me a squeeze before he settled.

CADE

Something woke me, but I wasn't sure what.

Lying there, Aspen tucked into my chest with my arms and legs wrapped around her, my body stiffened when I heard something just outside of the cottage bedroom window. A few seconds later—maybe ten or twelve—the distinctive sound of a doorknob being manhandled could be heard. It prompted me into action.

"Pen," I whispered.

Her eyes opened, and she tilted her gaze to meet mine. "What?" she said on a yawn.

"Someone's trying to get in," I explained with a finger covering her mouth, urging her to stay quiet. "I need you to go into your bathroom and lock the door. Don't come out until I tell you to."

"But—"

"We can argue about the fact that this is your place, and you're well and truly able to handle things on your own later. Now go."

She gave me a curt nod, then proceeded to get out of bed,

tiptoeing to the bathroom, but paused at its entrance to turn and face me. "Cade?" I looked her way. "Be careful."

With a silent nod, I watched as she closed the door behind her, then headed to check things out.

Giving Renegade the sign to stay, I was impressed when Molly followed his lead. Then again, having a ninety-five-pound dog practically sitting on you, in the dead of the night, would probably convince you to do that.

Exiting the room quietly, I could hear scraping at the kitchen window. It was as though someone was trying to jimmy the latch and slide the pane up to open it.

My emotions were flying at a new high, toying with me. I found myself struggling between two decisions: sit here patiently waiting for the perp to come in or go for the attack and risk having myself be found out and them escaping. As a man of action, it was laughable that I would consider the idea of hiding at all, but it still held merit. Waiting for a perp to enter would leave them with a harder time escaping when they'd been discovered and chose to run.

Thinking of the fact my woman had herself holed up in her bathroom—and I doubted she'd stay there until I returned—I opted to sneak out the front door as soundlessly as I could. I just didn't anticipate the fact the dogs would have an agenda of their own.

The instant the door opened, Molly made a mad dash, Renegade hot on her tail, both threatening masses of growling and barking fur.

Fuck!

Nearly bowled over, I regained my balance seconds later, and gave pursuit to the canines, hoping I could at least get a visual on the night's intruder. Making it to the side of the cottage, I managed a glimpse of a shapely silhouette—much the same as the one I'd seen a few days ago when I'd arrived back in town—only more distinctive and familiar which only served to confuse me further.

nineteen

Cade

BOTH DOGS WERE BACK within fifteen minutes, snarling and wrestling playfully with what turned out to be a frayed length of flannel.

Turning to head inside, I was tackled by Aspen, who came barreling through the front door and into my arms.

"Ren. Drop," I commanded. Molly continued to try and shred the material to pieces. "I'm okay, Pen." I ran my fingers through her disheveled hair, trying to calm her body's shaking.

"Did you see who it was?" she asked, as I dropped her on to her feet.

I shook my head, then turned toward Molly. "No. Molly, girl. Drop it." She kept it up. It would have been cute had it not possibly belonged to our mystery intruder. Seeing as the dogs got close enough to snag him, I was hoping it might contain some DNA or something substantive to tell us more about what we were looking at. Then again, that would only work if our perp was in the system at all.

"Molly. Leave. It. Now," Aspen commanded, and she finally did as asked.

Shaking my head, I crouched down to grab what was left of the material. On close inspection, I discovered I may have lucked out. "Gonna have that brought to Johnny in Raleigh and see if he can get one of his lab guys to run some tests for us. There's a little blood on it." I brought it up to show Aspen. "Got a Ziploc or a sandwich bag you haven't used and some tape to seal it?"

She nodded. "Shouldn't we go out there and look, though?" she asked.

"It can wait until morning," I told her, reaching for her hand and pulling her back toward the cottage. "First, I want to take care of this evidence. I'll have to take a sample of the dogs' fur to exclude those possible pieces of evidence too."

"But what if Molly and Renegade hurt them?"

I gave her a perplexed look. "Leave it to you to be the one wronged and still care about a person's well-being."

"It's not that." She sighed. "They might be slowed down by injuries," she explained, as we crossed the threshold. "If we went after them now, then we have a better chance of catching up, no? If we wait until morning, they'll most definitely be long gone."

"Babe." I smirked, pausing us by the couch. "I get what you're saying, but the worst thing to do right now is to go out there. It's got nothing to do with you and keeping you safe, sweetheart, trust me. In this case, I'd still advise the most well-trained person to stay put. Me included. The forest is dense around here, and in the pitch-black, even with a flashlight and a compass or GPS, it's quite easy to get turned around."

She groaned at that, then plopped onto the couch. "I know this area like the back of my hand."

"You might, but tell me this..." I paused, then crouched down so our faces were level before continuing. "This person has to be living remotely, just like you. That being said, have you ever spotted any shacks or other cabins in the area?" She shook her head to indicate the negative. Her nose scrunched up at that absolute fact, an indicator she disliked that I was right. "See? The area you know is nothing but a drop in a large bucket of trees and brush. Tomorrow, I'll call in a favor with the guys and see who we can rally up. We'll leave Molly at home so Renegade can do what he does best."

At that, Aspen perked up. "You mean I'll get to see him work?"

I laughed at her excitement and nodded. "Maybe. Now, I want you to go to bed. I'm going to secure this stuff, get the dogs in here, then check the kitchen window, and see what I can do to secure it. Now that they know we're here, not to mention the fact they might be injured, I doubt they'll be back to try anything tonight."

"Okay," she whispered.

Leaning forward, I gave her lips a chaste kiss and straightened up.

"If you need tools or extra wood..." She jumped up to her feet and headed for the kitchen, pulling out a drawer. She grabbed something from it, then came back to me. "It's all in the shed. Sandwich bags are in the cabinet under the sink." She dropped the keys she'd fetched in my waiting hand.

ASPEN

Before long, morning broke and my little cottage was teeming with testosterone. And I was pissed. Instead of being of use, Cade was sending me off on a beggar's errand with Devolin, once he'd called in a favor with one of his buddies at North Carolina's State Crime Labs in Raleigh.

"Don't you think I could be of more help here?" I asked, my hands on my hips. This was my place. My sanctuary was broken into, my privacy invaded, and I was going to fight to reclaim what was rightfully mine.

Cade looked over to Dalton, Brycen, and Rex in that universal manly language that begged for them to give him a minute. Pulling me to the side, he grabbed my upper arms and squeezed lightly. "Sweetheart, I need you to do this for us. I know you'd rather be here, but I can't tell you what we're going into or what we'll find...*if* we'll find anything out there. I want you clear of this if things go south. That means I need you to bring those bags to Johnny."

A short laugh, lacking any humor escaped me. "Cade—"

"Someone needs to get that piece of evidence to him." His eyes implored me to understand, and I did. I just didn't want to go, nor did I like it. With a sympathetic smile and a nod toward Devolin, who stood by Dalton's black Dodge Ram, he turned his eyes back to me. "Just think, you'll have a grand total of four hours of driving to talk Devolin's ear off about that hacking character you're wanting to write about."

That had me giggling, forgetting about my troubles for a few seconds as I reveled in the excitement of finally being able to have Devolin to myself to quiz her on the ins and outs of what she did best, but I knew what he was up to. "Sneaky bastard, you are, but true." I bit my lip lightly as the wheels in my head started to spin. "Can I ask you one thing though?"

Cade leaned forward and kissed my forehead. "Anything," he breathed his relief that I wasn't being more difficult.

"Will you call me if anything comes up? I don't care if you find anything or not, I just want to know you're all safe," I told him.

"Promise." His hand reached up to clasp the back of my neck. "Now kiss me, then get that sexy ass of yours gone so we can do our thing, and you can do what you do best, which is write that next best—"

I shut him up by smashing my lips to his. Pulling away, I pecked his scruffy chin. "See you soon." I backed away and turned, headed for Devolin and our ride.

"You seriously hacked into the government's satellites and pulled up those images to help the guys out?" My mouth dropped open as soon as Devolin nodded, sporting a wide grin on her face.

"Yup!"

What a crazy story she'd regaled me over the last forty-five minutes—the one where she initially met Dalton. To say I was feeling compelled to work a little of Devolin into one of my future characters was a gross understatement. She was definitely inspiration personified—and whether she agreed or not, she was going to be the lead in a new series that was beginning to take shape in my head—forget a simple singular character in only one book. This chick deserved an entire series featuring equally kick-ass women.

After a moment of silence, Devolin spoke up. "I have to say, you have me on pins and needles, with whatever it is you're planning, if you're asking me about what I do."

My laugh came easily, and I shrugged my shoulder in a noncommittal way. "So what other things have you done?" I deflected.

twenty

CADE

RENEGADE SEEMED LESS than impressed with me for tearing him away from his mate, but the moment his work vest had been strapped on, his demeanor changed as it always had. Damn I loved a well-trained canine.

On a long lead, the guys and I spaced out, radios in hand. We weren't forming a search grid per se. Being as we were a small group, it was easier for us to pull up a map and split things into quadrants.

It was barely past eight in the morning and the sun was rising farther, the midsummer heat climbing along with it as we set forth. Come hell or high water, we hoped to find answers before the day's end.

"Let's go, Ren." I headed us toward the entry point I'd seen the perp fade into, while the rest of the men did much of the same at a twenty to twenty-five-foot distance from one another.

. . .

"Got something," Rex's voice crackled through the radio.

It was after lunch. Last I'd heard from Aspen was that they'd reached Raleigh, and all was fine on the women's end. After four and a half hours in the bush, I was antsy to know more about what Rex had found.

"What you got?" Dalton's voice crackled through before I could say anything.

"You got a location?" I chimed in.

"Small shack. Not much left of it. East of you all," Rex paused, then proceeded to rattle off the exact coordinates.

Rex hadn't lied. By the time the team had reached the ramshackle remains of what had to have been a one-room shack—most likely for hunting—it was a smoldering heap of embers.

"Now what?" Brycen asked.

"We look through what we can to make sure no one was caught in this clusterfuck," I answered. "If we do, then we alert the authorities."

The men nodded.

Three hours later, we had nothing. If the place was where our perp had been holed up, then they'd made it out. Or they'd never been here to begin with. It had been impossible to even tell if anyone had been living there recently or not.

ASPEN

By the time Devolin and I returned, the men were still out. It wasn't until we stepped toward the cottage that I knew something was off.

First, my front door was left ajar, and I knew damn well Cade had locked it and still held the spare key on his person.

Second, Molly came simpering with a limp from around the back where the shed and chicken coop were located.

"The fuck?" Devolin took the words from my mouth. "The guys aren't back yet, or we would know it by now."

"No. You're right." I studied the front door, wondering what kind of chaos awaited me. "Someone would have called."

"Should we go in?"

I shook my head, indicating the negative. "Probably not, but I'm not staying here to wait on them. I—"

"We're two to their one," Devolin stated, walking back to the truck's passenger side door. Opening it, she reached in what I figured was most likely be the glove compartment. After closing and locking things up, she made her way back to me—gun in hand.

My body grew taut, eyes widening. "What the hell?"

"Relax," she smirked. "It's impossible to be married to Dalton and not know how to handle one of these babies. Not when the clan seems to keep growing and trouble lurks at every turn."

My body relaxed at her casual attitude, but my nerves were causing the lunch we'd eaten a few hours ago to churn about in my stomach. The woman sported some serious firepower for such a small revolver, and I hoped she knew it.

"Stay behind me," she ordered, then proceeded to head for the cottage, her right hand holding the weapon, the left supporting the butt of it.

I didn't bother to say anything. Instead, I took in the tiny sprite of a thing, the gun's safety off, weapon at the ready, looking like a serious badass.

Yeah, she's definitely going to be my next heroine, I thought, then shook myself out of the artistic mindset fog I had a tendency of falling into, because that wasn't where my head should be right then.

One minute, we're badass women on the prowl for my elusive B&E perp, the next, we're both too freaked out at what we'd seen, thus rushing out of the cottage, slamming the door behind us.

"What do you think this means?" Devolin asked, as she plopped down on one of the Adirondack chairs on my front porch, my ass collapsing into the one next to hers. "That shit is weird in there."

"What the hell did I take from them? I've never stolen so much as a fucking piece of candy, and even then, Mom made me bring the money to the store clerk to pay for it, after I'd apologized," I explained. "Don't let me get into what else I had to do in order to pay my mother back for that one."

Upon entering, it was clear that whoever had been inside my home had already left. The silence inside the small space was foreboding. Pillows had been shredded, books were scattered everywhere. My personal collection of my works had been shredded, page after page strewn everywhere, certain words circled. I was too shocked, and Devolin must have felt the same way, to even attempt to make anything out. Then again, she'd stopped me as I went to touch, warning me that it was all evidence, and until the guys got back, we shouldn't tamper with anything.

Most creepy of all had been the, *you took it away, now I'll take it from you* message and the second one, *give it back* that had been painted on my walls in something red, which I'd surmised to be some kind of paint. I never wandered toward my bedroom, not wanting to see any more of the chaos and destruction that awaited me.

"The guys are going to freak." Devolin was definitely right.

I nodded, then added, "We should have waited for them." As much as I hated admitting to it, the wreckage that was my cottage would have been better dealt with by someone else other than me. "I can't unsee any of that."

"Ladies."

On a shriek, both Devolin and I were out of our chairs, the only exception was that I was manning a bat while Devolin had her revolver pointed at Brycen, who hit the deck with a hard thud. Renegade barked up a storm at the man as he came running from the opposite direction Brycen had shown up from.

"The fuck?" came from Cade next, who nearly tripped over Brycen as he came running.

"Should have known you'd find trouble," Dalton stated as though this was a regular occurrence, taking large steps to his wife's side while he reached out with a, "Gimme the gun, woman." Once he pried the weapon from her grasp and tucked it in the back of his pants, he kissed her silly.

Meanwhile, Rex was leaning on the front deck railing, chuckling, Brycen was getting back to his feet, and Cade's questioning gaze was focused on me.

Dropping the bat to the floorboards, I ran and jumped into his arms with a muffled, "Someone's been in the cottage."

I was sure no one heard his breath catch, but I sure felt the tremor that wracked through Cade's body before it went rigid.

"Rex. Bryce. Check the cottage. Now," Cade ground out. "D and I will deal with the ladies." As he set me down on my feet, all it took was a single look in his eyes and I knew I was in for it —and not in a good way. A look over my shoulder toward

Devolin and her husband garnered me a wide-eyed expression from the woman in question that bordered an unneeded verbalized *oh shit*.

Yes, we had definitely stepped into the proverbial doo-doo.

twenty-one

CADE

"WHAT THE HELL were you two thinking?" Dalton roared. It might have been aimed to both women, but his eyes hadn't strayed from his wife. I'd only seen the man lose it a few times, and to be honest, he was scary as fuck—never violent though—and quick to defuse.

"Kip—" Devolin tried.

"What about Lucas? I got that gun in case you ever needed to defend yourself, baby." The man dropped in front of his wife and grabbed hold of her hands in his, shaking them in his grasp. "You're not supposed to use it for vigilante business. What if you'd been hurt... or died? Then what? How could I have explained that to our...our son...or your mom?"

"You should have stayed put in the truck and called us," I added, my gaze squarely on Aspen, whose eyes flared.

"And what?" she spat, but I could tell there was regret in her fiery gaze. As much attitude she was gearing to throw my way, I could tell she was shaken up by what she'd witnessed inside the cottage, and that alone had me bristling to hurry her away, tuck

136

her in the safety of my home, and never let her leave. "Was I supposed to let the beefy men handle my troubles like I always seem to be doing lately?"

I sighed, shaking my head. "Not what I meant, and you know it," I growled.

She snorted and rolled her eyes. "Whatever."

"Jesus, fucking Christ!" Brycen said, then slammed the door shut, and I could hear him tell Rex about his two whipped teammates, brought to their knees by their women, because by the time he'd attempted to walk out of the cottage, I'd taken up the same position Dalton had been in.

"I know that's not what you meant, Cade, but it doesn't negate the fact I'm being made to feel like the helpless little woman in all of this," Aspen said.

I leaned in to kiss her forehead. "I know, sweetheart. Believe me, I know."

"Dalton?" my woman added, then turned to the couple beside us. "I'm sorry. When Devolin grabbed the gun, I thought we'd be fine. I didn't even think about Lucas, or you. That's on me. Please don't be mad at her."

The man gave Aspen a small smile which turned genuine as though he was suddenly entertained again. "Women," he mumbled as he shook his head, his eyes aimed at his wife's knees.

No sooner, Devolin smacked him. "You'd be lost without me, Kip."

My boss was none too proud to admit it either. "Yes, baby, I would, which is why I'm certainly debating the merits of putting you in cuffs and throwing away the fucking keys."

"Just try it, Kip," she retorted. "And it wasn't Aspen's fault either. I have my own mind. Oh, we almost forgot! The dog needs to get checked out."

I had to admit it, Dalton knew when to stop arguing. His

point was made, Devolin knew it, understood it, and while she might not agree with his view, she knew she was his life and that's why she wouldn't push it either.

Fuck, but I want that. With Aspen.

"What's wrong with Molly?" I turned to the dog who'd taken up vigil beside us, Renegade at her side.

"She's limping. I think she must have gotten hurt when the break-in happened."

I cupped Aspen's face in my palm, then pecked her lips before giving her a sympathetic look. "Then let's get the guys to pack you both up, get to town, and see about a vet."

ASPEN

"But what about my cottage?" I demanded as Cade ushered me out the door, hurrying me to the passenger side of his truck, nudging me inside before shutting it behind me. "Cade?" He looked steaming mad. Evidently, my bedroom was something worse than I could have imagined. I wouldn't know. The guys never let me move past the entranceway.

"The guys will handle it." He slammed the rear cab door shut, after he deposited my overnight bag with enough clothes for a week, and my laptop case. He stormed back toward the house, nudged Renegade out of his way, then crouched to pick up Molly.

A minute later, the four of us were in Cade's truck, on our way to town.

Two minutes afterward, the man at my side grabbed my hand and laced our fingers.

"Let's get your girl looked after, then I'm picking us up some dinner." He sighed. "After we eat, we need to talk."

"What will the guys do?" Butterflies fluttered in my stomach. "Did you guys find anything out there?" My head reeled with so many things I wanted to ask, but if the look on his face was anything to go by, I wasn't going to get anything from him until he deemed it time to divulge something.

He shrugged his shoulders, then squeezed my hand. "They'll secure your place. Brycen's already placed a call with Stan to let him know what's happened. They're going to get some of the equipment Stan already has on hand installed. The man usually waits until all the equipment for an order has arrived before beginning an installation, but he's doing us a solid because whoever this is...they're escalating and that doesn't sit right with him, just like it doesn't with us."

"But—"

"I need the address to your vet," he cut me off. "We'll try there first. If they can't fit Molly in, we'll take her to mine."

"Renegade!" the receptionist exclaimed the moment we walked through the door. "How's my good boy?" Renegade rushed to her, tail wagging with happiness to see her, but his whining told her something was up.

I looked at Cade with amusement in my gaze. "Let me guess, Dr. Feinstein's your vet?"

The man in question made his appearance, his bespectacled face beaming at Cade's dog, but concern overrode his expression the moment his eyes settled on Cade cradling Molly in his arms. "Molly?" For the first time since he entered the room, the veterinarian looked my way. "What have we got here?"

"She was attacked. I think it's just a sprain," Cade explained.

The man nodded toward one of the open examination rooms. "Right this way. Don't you worry about a thing, Ms. Ridge. We'll get her feeling as good as new and ready to birth that litter of yours in no time." Smirking at Cade, as he sat my dog on the examination table, he added, "I take it Renegade is the father?"

Cade shrugged his shoulders and backed away to my side, wrapping an arm around my waist and grinned. "Guilty."

Renegade groaned, but stood sentry by the examination table, ensuring the good old doctor did all he could for his mate.

twenty-two

CADE

BY THE TIME we got home, Aspen had been going on and on about Dr. Feinstein's warning on getting things ready for Molly and the upcoming birth of her pups.

"We need the whelping box, and Dr. Feinstein reminded me I need to put together a kit in case of—"

Shoulders shaking, a smile on my face, I broke her soliloquy. "Sweetheart, I know we haven't talked much past the fact that Renegade knocked Molly up, but you're putting far too much worry in this whole puppy birthing business."

"Albert Caden!" Her eyes were as wide as saucers. "Have you not heard me? Seven fucking puppies are going to be shooting out of my poor innocent Molly in less than a month. Seven!"

I thanked my lucky stars we'd reached my driveway, because the tears of mirth began to fall as my laughter burst the dam.

"What's so funny?" She turned to face the windshield; her arms crossed defiantly over her chest. "None of this is humorous in the least. I'm thinking I should have never told

Feinstein that I'd handle things." Seconds later... "That's it, the minute she goes into labor, I'm bringing her in."

"Pen," I puffed out between bouts of hysterical laughter. "No need to worry."

"Seven, Cade. Seven!"

This had me in stitches once more, but the growl from the woman I had grown to adore in such a short amount of time had me sobering rather quickly.

"Sweetheart, I wish I'd known you were this worried," I told her, "but I've helped dogs whelp their pups before."

Her head snapped my way. "You have?" Her eyes scanned me from top to toe.

I nodded. "Renegade was actually from a litter I helped whelp," I explained, and grabbed for Aspen's left arm, smoothing my hand from her elbow to her wrist until I found her hand and pulled her crossed arms apart, entwining our fingers. "I even have the perfect spot for Molly's whelping box, but—"

Aspen's brows furrowed. "But?"

I shook my head, then reached over the steering wheel, turning the key in the ignition so the truck was off. "Let's take this inside. I think we can agree with how heavy today has been, a comfy couch, a drink, our dogs settled and comfortable will go a long way with us continuing this conversation. I'll order us something to eat."

"O—okay."

ASPEN

From the moment Cade pulled me from my seat in his truck, to the time we left the dogs, lounging on the carpet by the hearth, even when I'd settled against his side, a beer in both our hands,

I couldn't help but feel this day of heaviness hadn't completely blown over.

There was far too much to discuss; so many questions running amok in my mind.

What happened while Devolin and I had been on our evidence dropping run?

What else had the guys found in my place after I'd ran out like a spooked bunny, and they'd arrived?

Were the guys still at my cottage? Would it ever be safe again? Did I want it to be safe?

And why did Cade have a special whelping spot for my dog?

"I can hear those wheels turning in that beautiful head of yours, Pen."

"You said something about a special spot for Molly to give birth in?" I tried to pull away, but the arm he had around my shoulders kept me firmly wedged against him.

"Mm-hmm." He buffed his scruff over my head. "Yeah, but there's something else I wanted to talk to you about first."

My heart beat at a staccato in my chest. "Like?"

"Like what we found today, what the boys found after we left, and what they're up to at this very moment," he said.

This time, I pushed against Cade's chest, and he let me back away so I could sit up facing him, our knees touching. Before I could ask, he proceeded with telling me.

"We found a few patches of blood throughout the woods, but mostly, nothing more than an old burned down cottage. It couldn't have been more than ten miles from your cottage. It was far enough from you that you probably wouldn't have wandered there at all in your numerous treks. Shane's out there right now, searching the scene with some other detectives."

"Like I've said before, I haven't seen anything," I confirmed. "It was burned out?"

He nodded briskly. "Only just. Most of it was a mess of

smoldering embers when we got there. I'm thinking whoever was holed up in it set it on purpose. We didn't find a single remain, human or otherwise."

I nodded, but that's all I could do, my mouth having gone dry.

"The guys and I are in agreement that whoever this person is that's trying to get to you, they were probably staying there. It's either that or they set the blaze as a diversion to put some distance between us finding them. That's why there's still a search going on."

"But what do I have that's theirs?" I mumbled. "Cade, as much as I want to find this person, I can't help but think that whatever it is, they won't stop until they get their due."

Cade grabbed my beer and sat both our drinks on the table in front of us. "Sweetheart..." He grabbed my shoulders and pulled me back into his arms gently, our faces only inches apart.

"I know I've been eager to catch this person, and I know I've put up so much of a stink about being able to take care of myself but, Cade." I licked my lips, looking down from his eyes to gain a bit of fortitude. "Am I crazy for wanting to run and start fresh somewhere else?"

Pinching my chin, he tilted my head up so our eyes connected once more. "Explain. Now," he growled.

I sighed. "I don't want to fight for something that I feel I can't ever get back." I shook my head in his grasp, but my eyes stayed on his. "What I mean is, as independent and self-sufficient as I am, I'm not sure I'll ever feel safe in that place again, no matter how many doohickies Stan installs. It's not my safe haven anymore."

"What would make it your haven?" His voice came out smooth and deep, his eyes searching mine with...was it hope?

I shrugged, knowing it wasn't the answer he was looking

for by the light dulling in his midnight gaze. "I'm not sure, but I know it's not there anymore," I whispered.

"Right." When the look of determination entered his features, I knew that what would come out of his mouth next would floor me.

He certainly didn't disappoint.

twenty-three

"MOVE IN WITH ME."

My body jolted, but as I took in what I felt in that moment, it wasn't something akin to fear or uncertainty. It felt right. Too right for so early on.

"Aspen, just hear me out before you say something...please," he implored.

"O—okay," I sputtered.

"Where else are you going to go, a hotel?" he asked. "We're together, and in case you didn't get my last memo, I'm not letting you go until we see where this thing between us goes. You're mine, babe. I'm in it for the long haul, and you haven't given me any indication that you want otherwise."

"Yeah," I breathed. This man, though. Too. Good. To. Be. True. Through and through.

"We'll go ahead and secure the cottage. If you don't feel safe there, then fine, you don't have to go back. You need space, you have it. I've got three bedrooms in this place. I'll convert one into your dream office if that's what it takes."

I smirked at the picture of Cade, decked out in worn jeans, paint spatter everywhere, shirtless as he pieced together something to my tastes. Twirling my finger in the air, I said, "Keep going."

"We can keep the cottage and go back together as a change of pace; a way to escape life. Or you can sell it, and get something somewhere else, maybe the beach instead of the bush?"

I giggled. "The beach, huh?"

He nodded, but his lips never quirked upward. "Pen, I'm being serious here."

I sobered. "I know you are, honey."

Cade's eyes went molten. "It doesn't have to be permanent, and you don't have to make your mind up right away. But—"

The words were out of my mouth before I could process them. "I'll stay."

A whoosh of air tickled my lips. "Good," he breathed.

"Good," I repeated, grinning. "Cade?"

"Right here, sweetheart." His lips tugged upward at their corners.

"Kiss—"

Lips connected, and Cade reclined us so I lay over him. The feel of his erratically beating heart under my palm let me know that having me underfoot hadn't been an easy suggestion to voice, but it had been one he'd wholeheartedly wanted; which made this moment that much more colossal.

When I pulled away, I smiled at the man beneath me. "I know you said you'd build me the office of my dreams, but I think we'll be needing a chicken coop much sooner." I finished the latter on a hiccupped laugh.

"Anything for you, sweetheart," he rumbled on a chuckle, his hands soothing as they ran up and down my back.

Looking deep into his eyes, I knew he meant every word and then some.

. . .

CADE

Didn't she know I'd do anything for her? Now, more than ever, with the way I felt about Aspen Ridge, I'd give her the shirt off my back, my house, my money...my whole world.

Did I love her? I wasn't ready to let her know that giant factoid, but I sure as shit wasn't about to start lying to myself. I was utterly and completely in love with the woman currently nestled against my chest.

After her agreeing to move in with me, albeit on a temporary basis, she asked me to show her where I thought a coop for her chickens could be built. The playful twinkle in her eyes had me falling farther down into the abyss that was Aspen. Humoring her further, I even showed her where I'd envisioned an optimal location where Molly's whelping nest could be placed. Hell, I'd even brought her to the largest of the spare bedrooms. Based on the current design choices she'd made in her cottage, I'd started vividly painting a picture of what I thought she'd like, taking mental notes of her added suggestions. A woman like Aspen Ridge didn't make these types of suggestions if she wasn't serious about seeing where a relationship was going to go. Because she'd asked about a coop and had gone along with the office talk, I had a damned good inkling she was about as deep into this relationship as I was. Thank God!

After a little over an hour of ensuring my woman's decision to stay with me would stick—it hadn't been all that hard—we found ourselves cuddled on the patio's sofa, lounging with our second beers of the evening. The darkness of the night had washed over, and the stars shone above us. That's when my phone chimed from my pocket, disturbing our peace.

On a short giggle, thanks to the familiar showtune, Aspen snorted and said, "Better see what Brycen wants."

Instead of feeling the annoyance bubble at the stupid ring-tone I had yet to change—okay, so it was growing on me—I answered, "What you got, Babyface?" on a laugh.

"Just about to lock up. Mind if I stop by?"

My hackles rose. The man wouldn't suggest something like that if it wasn't necessary. "Come 'round back."

"Give me an hour or about. I have some things to load up first."

"Got it."

Aspen's body had gone rigid as soon as mine had. "What is it?" she asked as soon as I'd set my phone on the side table beside our drinks.

"Not sure, but I know none of it is good." Knowing her, sugarcoating things wasn't going to help me any. With my arm wrapped around her shoulder, I used my hand to soothe her arm, and added, "Let's not worry about it until it's time."

"Easy for you to say," she mumbled, but her body lost some of its rigidity even as she said it.

Brycen didn't show up alone. Two boxes apiece, the man was followed by Stan, Rex, and even Shane. Looks of fury and deter-mination were strewn across each of their faces.

"The fuck is this?" I gently pushed Aspen back on our seat and snapped to my feet. "I thought we'd agreed we'd get together tomorrow to pack up her things. All you had to do was bring the necessary items I gave you a list for."

"Get the door, tell us where you want this stuff, then we'll talk," Rex barked. Aspen's breath audibly caught from behind me.

Once I'd shown them a free spot against the living room

wall, I went back to my woman, and we waited for everyone to come back. I found her shaking, tears welling in her eyes.

"Pen?"

Without having to do anything myself, she crawled onto my lap and settled herself against me. She took deep breaths, then a few more, the tremors in her body subsiding with each passing second.

By the time she'd calmed, the guys had joined us, but none of them opted to say anything, looks of sympathy mixed with anger etched across their features.

"She's not going back there," Shane growled as he joined us.

"Fuck no," Rex shook his head vehemently, a storm brewing in the man's eyes.

"Aside from the furniture and household items, we packed what was still good," Stan stated, his earlier hardened expression having softened as he studied the woman wrapped around me like a petrified spider monkey. "I got the cameras up and running, but to be honest, with what I saw in there, and what we found after you all left, I'm thinking you'd be lucky if this person would let you escape with your life."

"W—what?" Aspen hiccupped, then turned so that her side leaned into my chest, my arms firmly still wrapped around her. She looked from one man to the next, but Shane spoke for the lot of them.

"Chickens were found, their heads ripped clean off," he stated. "That writing on the wall...chicken blood. Found one feathered beast next to that chair by the fireplace. Don't get me started with the rest. The mess alone is enough to give anyone nightmares. Jesus! From here on out, you don't just have NSI backing you, Aspen." Moving forward, he stuck his hand out. "Shane Peters, the JPD's been pulled in."

"Wish it were under better circumstances," Aspen took his hand with a shy smile. "You're the detective, correct?"

He gave Aspen a curt nod, released her hand, and backed up a few paces. "Yes, and I'm sure before the week is up, you'll have Devolin knocking at your door to introduce you to Emberlyn. If you're even luckier, they'll have Lana Rose and my mother trailing right behind them. They've been looking to add to their circle of estrogen." He winked at her.

I chuckled at that. When my eyes connected with his, I gave him an appreciative nod and said, "I just got her to move in with me until things get sorted out. Don't fucking scare her off now, man."

Brycen beamed. "If she can survive the likes of Devolin, Emberlyn will be a breeze, and little Rosie makes it all the more worthwhile. How is our little princess anyway?"

Shane turned to him and grinned. "Don't let her hear you call her little, princess, or Rosie. She'll have your balls, brother."

Rex laughed. "It's like that now, is it?"

Stan smirked. "Can't wait until mine gets a bit bigger, but I'm sure enjoying sleeping through the night now."

"My girl's a true firecracker." Shane beamed with pride. "Speaking of my ladies, I should get going. I promised them we'd have a family movie night. Their choice." He cringes as he says the last because we all know that between Rosie and Ember, those two were going to saddle him with some kind of chick flick that was suitable for a ten-year-old.

Twenty minutes later, with Aspen more relaxed and seeming to enjoy our unplanned guests, Rex, the last of the men, was making to leave.

"Thanks for everything, Rex," Aspen said, as she got up to give the big guy a hug which he returned. Despite her height, he dwarfed her, which was saying something about how monstrous the guy was.

"Honey, if you need anything at all, and your man ain't there to help out, I know all the guys would say the same, but promise me I'll be the first one you call," he rumbled. "Cade will make sure all \ our numbers are in your phone. Don't go anywhere without it."

"I won't," she said muffled into his chest.

"In the meantime, I'll be the one looking after your place. Gonna keep watch to see if that asshole comes back."

With a single nod against the massive man, Aspen let Rex go. My friend gave me a nod, then disappeared around the corner of my house.

twenty-four

OVER THE COURSE of the next week, Cade and I had found some sort of balance with our jobs and extracurriculars. It hadn't been all that hard considering he'd been called away on a search for a few missing campers, Renegade joining him, within a few days of my moving in.

He'd been gone for a little over forty-eight hours, but it hadn't stopped either Molly or me from feeling lonely in this large house we'd suddenly found ourselves living in.

The last two days Cade and Renegade had been around, and as the man had promised, he'd made sure I had the space I needed and time to work on my latest book. More often than not, with fall being around the corner and hurricane season on the horizon, I took advantage of the warm summer days and wrote outside. Sometimes Cade would join me, reading one of his numerous books. It was quickly becoming one of my favorite things. And on the days he was around, because he knew I was prone to forgetting to feed myself, he'd usually make me lunch and looked after dinner for both of us.

In the evening, we'd normally curl up together on his couch and watch a bit of TV before finding ourselves in bed, entwined in each other with a bout of robust sex. Tonight had been no different in that part of our routine, but there was an edge to the man currently crumpled overtop of me, our bodies plastered with sweat, his labored breathing puffing against my collarbone. It was an edge our first round hadn't really taken off on his side. Me, I was mellowed out and sated, but rile me up again, and I would take him and everything he would have to give me.

A minute passed, and when Cade didn't say anything, my mind began to wander.

Had I done something wrong? Did I not pick up on a cue of some sort? Did I forget to do something for him today, tonight... some time?

I'd taken care of the laundry earlier today. Was there something else I'd said I'd do and the thought of it simply escaped me?

Fuck, why do I suck at this part of a relationship so much?

I knew it wasn't about the sex. That had been something mind-blowing; tonight, better than the last time we'd been together. It was always better. Honestly, things had been insanely hot in that respect and had only gotten hotter every time we were together. I chalked it up to our budding connection on an emotional level. Never in my life had I thought about ways a man could complete me—complement my daily life— make me a better person, make my life that much brighter instead of it being shaded in undertones of gray and muted colors.

"Sweetheart?" Cade's voice knocked me out of my musings.

"I love you," came flying out of my mouth before I could think better of it.

His body jackknifed upward. Cade's jaw ticked as he bore

his weight on his elbows, his lower half beginning to harden once more inside me. His eyes deepened with emotional intensity, to the point of looking entirely black instead of their regular turned-on midnight blue. "What did you just say to me?"

I was sure my eyes had gone wide. "Holy shit, Cade." Then my mouth did that thing it had just done and ran away from me some more. "I'm sorry! I shouldn't have said it." I shook my head from side to side. This couldn't be it. I just had to be this inept at a relationship that I caved to the sexed-up woman trope that gave those three words to a man after he'd rocked her world. "It's so fast. It's—"

A hand covered my mouth, causing my wandering eyes to fuse to his, and that's when my panic ebbed, my body going limp.

"I'll be fucking dammed," he whispered, his irises going liquid. "She beat me to it."

"Hmph?" was all I could manage behind his large palm.

With his eyes searching mine, he shook his head. "It's right there. It's been there this whole fucking time, and I didn't see it until just now."

"Mmmph."

"Motherfucker!" Pulling his hand away, his mouth replaced it in a soul-shattering kiss. His body shook as if it were at the point of breaking, and I found myself wrapping my arms around him, cradling Cade as if he were the most precious thing in my life, and I was the one responsible for holding him together.

CADE

I don't think I've ever been this fucking hard in my life. A week. A single week of us living together was all it had taken for Aspen to tell me she loved me. I'd suspected it with the look I'd occasionally spotted in her eyes over the last few days. It had been the same one I'd seen my mother give my father over the years, before things had gone south. I had simply never seen it directed toward me until this past week.

Love.

Aspen loved me.

And I loved her.

To be honest, I'd been wracking my brain on how to let Aspen in on my feelings since the night I asked her to move in. I knew she didn't have much experience with serious relationships, and her independent streak was a mile wide compared to the other women I'd dated. Then, there was the fact that aside from family, I'd never given those words to another soul. Considering her past hurts, I knew Aspen Ridge was an enigma who had only let a handful of people see the real her, and I was one of the lucky bastards to witness those guards of hers come down. And boy had they crumbled tonight.

Tearing my mouth from hers, I finally let her see all of me.

"You wreck me, Pen," I said, my breath coming out in hard pants. "You undo me at every turn, and this moment, this one right here," I paused to swallow the surge of emotions threatening to clog my airway, "is what I've been living for my entire life. I fucking love you, Aspen Ridge. Without a doubt. No reservations. It's what I know in my heart of hearts, and if you let me, I'll make sure to guard yours. You'll never regret giving me those words, sweetheart. They're mine and you can't have them back." I punctuated the last of my words with another deep kiss, this one unhurried...gentle—one meant to cherish.

She was mine.

I was hers.

Nothing or no one would take this from me—from *us*.

Encased in the cocoon that was Aspen's arms and legs, I proceeded to show her the depth of my devotion with my body, the tension that had been there during our first round having fully dissipated, because I'd been true to my feelings and had finally let the final wall crumble.

twenty-five

THAT TELLTALE chirp from Cade's cell came through the light of early dawn. As I lifted my head, I caught an image on the phone's screen that had shivers creeping up my spine.

Careful not to jostle a clearly depleted and exhausted Cade, I shuffled myself away from his prone body, grabbed one of his old T-shirts, hurrying to get it on, then padded to his bedside table to grab the phone. By then, I had to hit the home button in order to activate the screen, but what I saw had my balance faltering.

Beneath Rex's "What's our girl doing at her cottage?" was a short video footage of *me*.

Except it wasn't. The timestamp would disprove that, considering that at 5:56 a.m., I'd been in the middle of slumbering slumped over the man I'd finally professed my love to only last night. A man who felt the same way.

Not wanting to invade more of Cade's privacy, I set his phone back where I'd grabbed it, then tiptoed out of the bedroom.

There was no way I'd be able to fall asleep again.

Reality hit with trepidation as the slight click to the bedroom's doorknob echoed in the otherwise quiet house.

It can't be, can it?

The moment I pulled out of the driveway, regret bubbled in my stomach, but the urge to solve the question nagging in my gut was larger. So much so that it overwhelmed rational thought outright.

When I pulled on to the gravel stretch that led to my cottage, my sense of urgency was so potent, despite the fear emanating from my every pore, I kept forward.

I just hoped Cade would forgive me this once for leaving his bed, leaving his house, and taking Renegade with me. I'd left Molly at home though. I'd also packed along the small, fully loaded 9mm Ruger, with an extra magazine, that Cade kept stashed in a locked cabinet in his front closet. The day after I'd moved in, my man had taken me to the shooting range and shown me how to use it, telling me where the keys were in the event I found myself in danger and without any manpower to help me out.

I was pretty sure this wasn't one of those times he'd ever recommend my borrowing it though. In fact, I knew it wasn't.

"Now, Ren," I ruffled his ears. "You ready to work, boy?" I hit the glove compartment button and snatched the handgun and its compatible clip.

Renegade's ears perked up. I figured there wasn't any harm in suiting him up in his work vest either, just to get his mindset right. I'd learned a few tips and tricks thanks to researching my past novels, but in the last week under Cade's roof, I'd seen how he and Renegade's work relationship functioned.

"Quiet."

I had parked the car some distance from the cottage, so that if who I'd seen in the video was still around, I wouldn't be made from the get-go.

Opening the driver's side door, Renegade followed suit. Tucking the clip into the back pocket of my jeans, I decided to keep the gun in my hand, but the safety would stay on for the time being.

Heading into the copses of trees lining the rest of the drive, and almost touching the right of the cottage, I crept, ever so careful not to make a noise, watching out for the copperheads, eastern diamondbacks, or any other slithery critters that were native to our area.

When I reached the edge of the woods right next to my cottage, I breathed a sigh of relief for not being found out. If Stan had done his work well, I knew there'd be no hiding. That fact alone had my current apprehension fading. I might be out here, armed with some firepower and a trained K-9, but the fact I was about to be on video would prove where I was and at what time.

I'd just made it to the porch steps when Renegade whined, and an explosion of pain burst into the back of my head. Then all went black.

CADE

Honey,

Just stepped out and took Renegade for a little bonding time.

I'll be back for breakfast.

Love always,

Pen

To say I was shocked to wake up entirely by myself was one thing. My woman having not only left our bed, but also our home so early in the morning after we'd professed our love to each other had me a little miffed if I'm being honest.

Seconds after reading the note she'd left by the coffee pot, which had been percolated and left full, I heard my phone's chime go off.

There was only a few reasons my phone would go off at this time of day. Seeing as I was on an extended weekend from my regular day job, it was either Nightshade calling me in, my mother or sisters with an emergency—or Aspen.

The last person on my mental list had me rushing to my phone, thankful that when I saw Devolin's number and activated the call, I was smiling into the line.

"Hey, well, if it isn't my favorite half of the Kippers clan. Up a little early for someone with a little guy at home on a lazy Saturday morning, aren't you?"

"We've got trouble," she said all businesslike.

My hackles rose as I heard shuffling on the other end of the line. "Huss, what's going on?" I demanded, using her hacker monicker.

"Where's Penny... I mean Aspen?" she asked almost accusatorily.

"Just got up and saw her note, but she's gone out and should be back by—"

"Wrong."

"The fuck?"

"Lucas doesn't sleep much at night, and since Rex has been burning the midnight oil, I opted to relieve him over the weekend and stand sentry on Pen's cottage footage. Clocked her no less than five minutes ago, and you're not going to like this, but there's two of them."

"What?"

"There's—"

"I heard you, Dev, but why didn't you call as soon as you saw her?"

"Because I thought I'd give her the chance to regain some of her brass since she's said that she was terrified of going back there. I changed my mind when I thought of you, how worried you were last week when—"

"And Ren?" I asked, as I began to slide my legs into yesterday's jeans, not caring the state of the crumpled T-shirt I manage to slide over my head as I waited for her answer.

"Don't know," she said with worry in her tone.

Shoving my feet in the sneakers by the closet, I grabbed my truck keys, then made my way to the front door, slamming it shut behind me. "Dev, I need you to call in the cavalry. Make sure Shane is part of the clan and brings in the official brass while he's at it."

"Got it."

Jumping into my truck, I jabbed the ignition with my key and cranked it to life. "If anything else comes up, let me know." I didn't bother telling her there were quite a few dead zones for cell reception in the area I was headed, because the woman was a computer genius and she'd most likely figured it out long before now anyway. Hell, I wouldn't put it past her to find a way to boost tower signals just to be able to get a call to go through. Or a message.

Without waiting for a response, I hit the *end* button and dropped my phone in the middle console.

twenty-six

REX

WHEN I FIRST SAW THE footage and Cade didn't respond to the text message I had sent him, I'd never been more thankful for Devolin's call offering me relief of my watchdog duties. I told her that under no circumstance was she to take her eyes off the screen. With that, I had gotten my ass in gear and headed straight for Aspen's cottage. I never told Dev what was going on, sure she'd figure things out in due time.

I also tried to dial Aspen's cell, but her voicemail picked up immediately, telling me that it had either been turned off, or her battery had run dry.

Fucking women and their fool heads!

As I tore up the highway, driving like a bat out of hell to get there in less than the forty minutes it would take the average driver to reach my destination, something wasn't sitting right. The footage I'd witnessed earlier played in a constant loop in my mind, and even though I knew something was off, I couldn't pinpoint what it was.

The moment I got to the cottage's turnoff, I pulled off the

road, parked, and decided to go the rest of the way on foot, making sure I had my Beretta tucked in the waistband of my pants.

I passed Aspen's vehicle, glad to see she'd had the common sense of a true investigator, but that all went to shit when I observed her out of the tree line, making her way toward the porch.

Anyone could have seen her from any direction, which is what happened.

One minute, she was crouched by the front door, the next, I witnessed Aspen hitting Aspen with a two-by-four at the back of the cranium, my own head reeling at the image.

There's two of them?

The next thing I knew, the unkempt version of Aspen was pulling her doppelgänger by her underarms into the cottage, and my gaze settled on Renegade, cowering back into the bushes where they'd probably come from.

Yeah, I'd be confused too, buddy.

When the door to the cottage slammed shut, that's when I made my move.

CADE

I was unsure as to how long it took me to make it to Aspen's cottage, but I sure felt the sense of relief I wouldn't have to wait for backup when I spotted Rex's Suburban off the side of the road.

Pulling in behind him, I headed for the trees, sure of the way I'd planned on sneaking up on whomever it was I'd come up on when I'd reached my destination.

The phone in my back pocket vibrated. Halting my progress,

I pulled it out and unlocked the screen to reveal numerous full-length texts.

DEV:

Men on the move.

Rex on scene.

Another ping.

SHANE:

On route. Coroner report came in on that vic from the skip you helped Rex with. Talk when this bullshit with this perp is over and Aspen is safe. Hold tight.

DEV:

Rex on his way to you.

Minutes later, I heard the low whistle we'd used as a call sign with one another on previous missions.

Seconds after that, Renegade was at my side with Rex emerging shortly thereafter. My four-legged partner wasn't the jovial mutt he always was, his ears back and low on his head, his gaze aimed downward as though he felt like a failure.

"There's two of them," Rex first said.

"Two perps, got it." His message nothing new to what I'd gotten from Devolin.

Although frustrated, his eyes held disbelief. "No, man, two Aspens."

"The fuck?"

"Didn't you get my text at the ass crack of dawn?" he asked.

I shook my head, pulled my phone back out and went to my message app. That's when I caught a text I'd missed simply because it had already been read.

Aspen.

Opening it, I saw the message and immediately knew he wasn't talking out of sleep deprivation or some sort of hallucination. The video footage also went a long way to explain why she'd taken off like she had.

But I knew the difference immediately.

"Fuck me." I let out a string of additional expletives, shoving my phone back in my pocket and raking my hands through my hair. "Goddamn it, Pen!" I whisper-yelled.

When all of this was over, I was sure to tan her perfectly pert hide.

"Not the time, Cade," Rex growled. "I just saw your woman get clocked hard with a chunk of wood. At best, she's got a lump to rival the size of a fucking ostrich egg; at worst, she's got one hell of a concussion, or she's—"

"Don't even fucking say it," I growled.

The man's hands came up in a peacekeeping manner. "You ready to go then?"

With one nod, we set off, me in the lead, Renegade at my side, and Rex manning my six.

Aspen

My ears were ringing.

My head throbbed as if someone had stuck it in a blender.

My pulse raced, and I was struggling to keep my churning stomach from rebelling and me losing what was left of last night's dinner on the floor I was currently crumpled on.

Taking a few calming breaths, hoping to all hell I wasn't being obvious of my being conscious, I wanted to get my bearings long enough to assess the extent of my injuries and figure out where my attacker was.

I needed a plan.

I felt eyes on me, so I knew whoever it was that hit me earlier was in the room with me. The pungent smell of disinfectant, that most likely was a fragment from when the Nightshade crew had been in here, mixed with stale air and what I could tell were the remnants of one of my apple-cinnamon candles in the air, let me know I was in what used to be my safest place on Earth.

"Wake up, bitch!" A swift kick to my ribs had me shrinking into a ball on the hardwood surface.

"W—why?" I croaked, trying to take a deep breath in, but unable to do so, due to the pain in my right side, so I straightened myself out a bit to take pressure off my middle. I was pretty sure she'd at least cracked a rib. "What do I have—"

"You took it away!" the female voice, so similar to my own albeit slightly unused, hollered as she kicked me once more. "You took it all from me, and I can never have it back."

Any doubts I had about bruising, or a simple fracture, were washed clean out of my mind when I heard the telltale cracking sound. My next breath inward had stars exploding behind my eyelids and fire streaking through my lungs.

Trying to conserve what strength I had left, and keeping myself safe, I no longer cared how hard it was to breathe. For self-preservation purposes, I curled myself in the fetal position, giving her less surface area to make contact with.

"You could have saved him! I wouldn't be alone if it wasn't for your choice to pick him over me," my attacker rambled on. "He gave me everything! From the time I was a little girl, he was my only friend."

Any doubt of what I'd seen in the short video footage on Cade's phone vanished.

"W—Willow?" I coughed, and when I tasted blood, I knew I was in trouble.

"Don't call me that! I haven't been Willow in twenty-five years."

It really is her?

Now, it all made sense. The way I felt closer to her by moving into the cottage when I'd thought all along it was because she'd disappeared in these same woods, albeit a much farther distance from here. The hope that had always been there, that I would find her again someday.

But any hope that some sort of sisterly relationship would be able to be rekindled with my sister dissipated the moment our eyes connected for the very first time since the day when the man had taken her away from my parents—from me. Willow was dead. In her place resided some wild and hollow being who had an axe to grind, and for the life of me, I can't put two and two together to make four.

"Abe is gone and I'm all alone."

"He took you from us," I struggled to get out.

"He took me and gave me the best life I could have ever hoped for, and that man you've been fornicating with, writing that filth about, took him away," Willow accused. "Just like it was when we were kids. It was always you over me. That's why I went with Abe. It's why I never wanted any of them to find me. But you ruined it, and once I'm done making you pay for taking away the only thing I love, he'll be next."

"Wil—That won't make the pain go away," I croaked. Closing my eyes, trying to stave off the dam of tears threatening to flow out of sadness and desolation, I remembered the gun tucked in my front left side of my jeans, covered by my shirt. I reached slowly for it but came up empty.

"Looking for this?" My eyes snapped open to find Willow holding Cade's weapon in her hand. "You seriously didn't think I wouldn't look for anything that could be used against me while you were out, did you?"

"Y—you don't need to do this." I tried to sound confident, but it came out as a whisper.

Next thing I knew, my world exploded with fear as I saw Cade's face flash through the window above the kitchen sink at Willow's back.

I'd been found, but if he came in here, Willow would do to him exactly what she had planned. And I didn't doubt that she would take the shot to get to him, even before she'd be done with me.

Putting every ounce of strength into my voice, I yelled a pitiful sounding, "No!"

CADE

I about lost my mind the moment I heard Aspen screaming, "No!" through the door. I'd barely felt the crumpling of the wooden barrier when I crashed through it, Rex at my back. Frankly, I had already lost my shit as soon as I spotted the blood under her head, while she lay in the fetal position, her face contorted with pain.

The only thing I hadn't noticed, because the perp's back had been to me and the window I'd quickly glanced through, was the fact she had been brandishing a weapon, one that had been trained on my woman up until two seconds ago.

"Oh fuck, no!" Rex shouted about the same time Renegade lunged past me and tackled the crazed woman.

"Get Ren off and I'll secure her, then you can go to your woman," Rex ordered loud enough to be heard over the screeching banshee.

"Renegade, release!" I said, as I hurried to check Aspen out, confident my dog would do as he was trained. When I skidded to a stop in front of her, the up-close sight had me wincing.

Although she looked as though she slept, I knew she'd passed out from the pain. The fact her face was still contorted in a grimace, and her arms, although limp, were still wrapped around her middle had me wondering if I should even attempt moving, let alone touching her at all.

Seconds later, Renegade came to lay in a whimpering mess at my side, a safe distance from us. Rex had managed to take the power cord from a lamp he'd cut off with the help of his utility knife and had secured the bitch who'd done far more damage to Aspen than I'd ever thought possible.

"This isn't over!" she shouted. "You'll lose everything you took from me. I promise you that!"

"It is for you," Rex spat, as he whipped out his cell and began dialing. The moment he finished barking out our location, he hung up, then hit a button on his phone. "Yeah... We got her... She's fuckin' banged up bad... Ten-four." Pocketing his phone, he explained, "The cavalry just got here. They're jumping back in their vehicles and coming up the drive. Ambo is right behind them along with the cops."

I could only nod my response, the lump in my throat impeding the possibility for words.

When I turned to face Aspen's tormentor, I was floored by her unkempt nature, but also by the fact that she looked almost identical to my woman. It was unsettling how I could love Aspen so much, then face a person, nearly her mirror image, and hate her with the fire of a thousand suns.

twenty-seven

Aspen

I CAME to as Willow was making an attempt to escape Rex and Shane's grasps while the men were trying to help the uniformed officer exchange what looked like an electrical cord for handcuffs.

I'd read about people who lived in the wild and off the land, hunting and fishing for their food, harvesting random things in order to make clothes and so on, but not once had I ever thought my sister, a member of society for the first eight years of her life, would have turned into something akin to a wild, untamed animal. And that was what I was witnessing at that very moment.

"Where does it hurt, sweetheart?" I heard Cade's voice through the chaos.

"Everywhere," I croaked. "Think my ribs are broken. Heard... a...cracking snap." I paused to breathe. "Hurts to breathe. Fire."

"Okay." He leaned over me and kissed my forehead. "We've got the medics on the way. Is there something I can do to make things better? Can you move a bit? If you stretch out, it'll help with the breathing."

It took me a minute to get settled, and I breathed better, but holy shit had it hurt like hell. "My head is pounding. I think she hit me pretty hard."

"Yeah," he whispered. "Any nausea?"

I tried to nod, closing my eyes as a bout of queasiness became overwhelming, so I swallowed hard.

"Concussion," I heard someone else say, thinking it sounded much like Rex.

"Punctured lung," another said, Shane this time I thought. "She's coughed up blood."

"Keep talking," I told them. "Don't wanna...sleep."

"Got it, sweetheart," Cade promised. "Just rest. We'll keep you entertained."

"Renegade?" I croaked.

The dog in question whined and then I felt him nudge my foot. As if he knew everything above the waist hurt something fierce, he covered my shins and lay over me. His heat a welcome blanket that soothed.

"S—sorry, boy," I managed.

"Shh," Cade ordered. "Just rest and concentrate on breathing. Renegade is safe and so are you."

Cade

If I were ever one to lift a hand against a woman, hearing the words out of Aspen's mouth about where she hurt and witnessing the difficulty she had with expressing herself would have been enough for me to put a beating on so good, the other woman would never forget it.

Aspen lost the battle with staying conscious moments after

Renegade covered her legs with his body. The medics were just pulling up, and Shane's JPD coworkers were trying to extract information from our otherwise uncooperative perpetrator.

"Willow," I barked, following my gut. "You're fucking Willow Ridge, aren't you?"

"Not that I owe you an answer, but I'll tell you the same thing I told that bitch, I haven't answered to that name in over twenty-five years."

"If you don't want me to add resisting arrest to your current charges of kidnapping, battery and assault, and breaking and entering, along with whatever else I can make stick so you go away for a long-ass time, I suggest you fucking cooperate," Shane ordered, yanking Willow to her feet, then urging her forward. "Get her out of here and get her processed."

Standing back to give the medics room to work, I gave my detective friend a curt nod, but not once did I remove my eyes from Aspen as the health professionals proceeded with sliding a C-collar to stabilize her spine, then they put her on a backboard.

"You okay, man?" Brycen asked from one side, Rex on my other, with Renegade next to him. We all stood sentry over the working man and woman team currently trying to insert a line in my girl's arm so they could deliver some fluids and pain meds.

"Pupils blown out," one called into their shoulder radio. "BP one thirty-two over ninety-six. Shallow breathing. Painful on the right torso. Five minutes to loading. Thirty-five minutes out."

"Sorry, men, but we need to get her on the stretcher," the man told us.

Moving out of the way, I watched as they moved Aspen from floor to stretcher.

"Go with our girl," Rex said.

"We've got your truck covered," Brycen added, squeezing my shoulder. "We'll meet you at the hospital."

As the medics headed with a strapped-in Aspen, I followed suit. "Boy, stay with Rex," I called over my shoulder without looking back.

By early evening, I was still in the waiting room, the rest of the guys, Devolin, Emberlyn, and Lana Rose having joined me. I knew some of the extent of Aspen's injuries since she'd told me about them herself, but what else had the doctors and nurses discovered during their examination? Had there been any complications?

Every time someone in scrubs and a stethoscope came out, I'd gotten up, hoping it was news I was destined to hear. It hadn't been.

I paced the waiting room, currently on cup of coffee number five, my body telling me it had fallen victim to three cups too many with my current jitters. I hadn't eaten the sandwich Emberlyn and little Rosie had brought for us either, too amped up with not knowing anything. Brycen had dug into that extra pastrami on rye with little hesitation.

We were the only group left in the waiting room when finally, the set of doors I'd been focused on all day flew open, and a woman, not much older than us came through.

"Family of Aspen Ridge?"

"Here," I said, then let the lady doc approach. "Fiancé. Caden Summers. How is she, Doc?"

"Well, Mr. Summers, she's got a severe concussion, two broken ribs, a punctured lung, and quite a bit of bruising." My stomach dropped as she listed Aspen's injuries. "She'll be in a great deal of pain, and right now, we're having issues with waking her. She's not making much sense, but that's normal."

"When can we see her?" Rex asked, coming to my side, setting his hand on my shoulder.

"I—I don't think it's wise to have too many visitors in these first twenty-four hours," she said, but her eyes were glued to Rex, whose hand stiffened on me, causing me to shift beneath his grip.

"Sorry, man," he rumbled, but his words were distracted, his eyes locked on the woman standing across from us.

If I wasn't worried about Aspen and needing to see for myself that she was okay, I'd find this entire scene quite entertaining.

"Ms. Ridge needs her rest, but as you're her fiancé, Mr. Summers, we'll make an exception," the doctor stated, then eyed the rest of our group. "As for the rest of you, I'm not changing my mind," her eyes settled and focused with intensity on Rex, "and that's that. Come back tomorrow and depending on how my patient is doing, I might just let you through to see her, two at a time. Come on, Mr. Summers, I don't have all day."

Turning on her heel, she disappeared right where she'd come from a little more hurried than what I figured was her normal.

"Damn," I heard Rex say under his breath, causing me to chuckle.

"On that note, I'll keep you all posted." I hurried after the doctor.

When she pointed to the doorway she stood next to, I could tell the woman was a little off-kilter after that short interaction with Rex.

"About my friend out there," I started.

"Don't worry about it," she mumbled. "Visiting hours end at ten."

"I'm not leaving, Doc," I told her. "She's been through hell and back, I'm not going anywhere. I'll be quiet, I won't disturb anyone. Hell, you won't even know I'm there, but I either park my ass on those plastic chairs out there in the waiting room, or the comfier version of them in the room with her. Your pick."

With her arms crossed over her chest, she still didn't have as strong a stubborn streak as my Aspen.

On a huff, she capitulated. "Fine. Stay. I've got patients to check on, and I'd rather be doing that than standing here arguing with you."

"Glad we're on the same page, ma'am," I muttered to nothing but air; the doctor having already left.

twenty-eight

ASPEN

THE INCESSANT BEEPING OF A MONITOR, the smell of antiseptic, and the hard as a rock bed beneath me were great indicators that I was still trapped in my nightmare.

The pain radiating and burning in my chest, the sensation of an elephant sitting on it, and the sharpness of each breath were all telling me I was alive, and I'd never been more grateful.

The last thing I remembered was seeing Cade's face, but I wasn't certain if I'd been dreaming after having spotted him outside of the cottage and losing my mind over the fact he was walking into danger.

I took a shallow breath and licked my dry lips, aware there was someone in the room with me, but I simply couldn't make my eyes open just yet. "Please tell me," I inhaled once more, "it's over."

"I have half a mind to lock you up and throw away the key with how you scared us," I heard Rex say. "How're you feeling, honey?"

"Rex?"

"Last I checked." His laugh was deep, low, and smooth. I liked the sound coming from such a rough-looking man.

"Where...where's Cade?"

"Went home for a shower," he explained, then I felt his hand wrap around mine. "He's been here for nearly forty-eight hours. I sent him home to freshen up. Doubt he'll be away for much longer."

"Mmm," I croaked. "I have a jackhammer in my head."

"Need meds?"

"Please."

"Let me get the doc. They'll want to know that you woke on your own for once."

Staying still, I waited no more than thirty seconds before I heard Rex's steps return to my bedside, another twenty or so before another set made their way toward me.

"Ms. Ridge?" I felt a dainty hand barely touch my shoulder. "I'm Dr. Reina Boudreaux."

"Hi," I mumbled.

"I know you're hurting, but can you open your eyes for me?"

I did as she asked, wincing, closing my eyes momentarily, and it was as if someone had read my mind, because behind my eyelids I felt the lights dim then heard the curtains close at the windows.

I tried again.

"Good. Can you tell me your name, age, and what got you here?" the doctor asked. I gave her what she asked, and over the next few minutes, she proceeded to ask me where it hurt most, checked my vitals, then came the hard part.

"Oh shit," I cursed, as she helped me sit up a bit.

"Now that you're properly conscious, we need to get you started on your breathing exercises to ensure your lungs and ribs heal correctly," she explained. "It's not going to feel great, but it'll get easier with time. I want you to repeat these deep breathing exercises every hour. Just a few deep breaths. The pain meds should help with making them bearable."

"'kay," I said, and started my first set of two.

"So I've been out for two days?" I asked Rex when the doctor had at long last left, and the nurse had popped by for a dose of painkillers that only took the edge off.

He nodded. "You woke up, but you'd mumble something, then fall right back to sleep."

"I don't remember any of that," I paused. "Is everyone okay?"

"They're all worried about you, especially Cade, but we're all good," he assured me. "Do me a favor, though." He didn't wait for me to agree. "Keep out of fucking trouble from here on out. Not sure my man Cade's heart can take it."

For the first time since I'd woken up next to Cade, then seen that video on his phone, I smiled. "Promise."

CADE

It took far too fucking long to get back to Aspen. For what should have been a trip home to shower, change, and get refreshed, packing a few items of my girl's for when she woke up, I should have known that something would pop up.

When Shane called to let me know he was sitting on the coroner's report for the man who'd plummeted to his death during that skip retrieval gone wrong, which had led me to the love of my life, I knew I needed to see it.

As it was, we now knew the John Doe's case linked with what had happened to Aspen, as Willow had finally broken and told the investigators what she'd done and why she'd done it all.

Jealousy.

Love.

Loyalty.

Grief.

I also discovered that Abe—or Abraham—Grennich, had priors relating to attempted child abduction and a few misdemeanor charges. He was one of those one-percenters—a survivalist—living off the grid, in a bunker of his own making. It explains a hell of a lot as to why Willow had never been located. After multiple attempts, we knew the exact location where his bunker's entrance was—it so happens to have been thirty or so feet from where the burned-out shack once stood. Who knew if Grennich had abducted more kids after he'd been incarcerated, whether it had been before or after he'd taken Willow Ridge. And if he had, where the hell were they? If they'd perished, why hadn't anyone found bodies? She certainly hadn't indicated if she'd been the only one or not, but Shane and his crew would be investigating things starting today, and I looked forward to putting the rest of this nightmare in the past.

By the time I made it back to the hospital, I'd stopped at one of my favorite delis to pick up some lunch for Rex and myself. I'd even picked up a little something for Aspen, in the event she woke up. I hated the fact she hadn't been coherent over the last two days, and honestly, I was worrying myself sick, wondering what kind of mental state she would be in when she finally did. Brain injuries weren't out of the realm of possibilities where severe concussions were concerned.

Hurrying toward Aspen's room, I found myself smiling when I heard Rex's voice. They'd kept visitors to one at a time until further notice, but if he was conversing, that only meant—

"Promise," I heard Aspen's soft voice as my hand met her room's door, which was open a slight crack. I pushed it inward.

"The only promise I want to hear is you're hurrying your ass up to heal and get out of here so you can come back home to me," I ordered, but I couldn't hide the joy from my expression. "Sandwiches all 'round." I lifted my bag of goodies, handed it to Rex and headed for Aspen's side, kissing her lightly on the forehead. "Got you a little something too if you're feeling up to it."

"I love you," she blurted. As soon as she realized she'd said it in front of company, her face flushed that beautiful crimson I'd missed over these last few days.

"Good to know," Rex mumbled, as he busied himself with his food container.

Leaning down so our eyes were level, I gave it to her honest. "I love you too, sweetheart, but don't kid yourself, when you're feeling better, we'll be having a discussion about you leaving our bed without my knowing."

She smirked, grabbed on to the front of my shirt and pulled me closer. "Sounds deliciously devious," she whispered, right before she laid a fast one on me, then pushed me away with horror on her face. "Sorry! My breath is probably horrendous right now."

"You think I give a shit about that?" To prove it, I slammed my mouth down on hers, taking my time until Rex cleared his throat.

"Guys, I'm famished, but you keep at it, and I'll be losing my lunch shortly."

Pulling away, I press my head to her forehead. "Fuck me, but I missed that mouth," I said.

"Again...still here," Rex whispered loudly. "Or did you forget I hear almost every damn fucking thing?"

"Fucking owl," I mumbled, but went in for another swift kiss, nonetheless, before pulling back and reaching for both our food containers. "Sweetheart, you want to try sitting up a bit more?"

On a "yes" that was mixed with an anticipatory wince, I grabbed the bed's controller and handed it to her.

"You control how fast and far you go," I said.

"Is that what you told her the first time too?" Rex asked through a mouthful of food.

Aspen hissed out as she tried not to laugh.

"Fucker," I growled. "Don't make her laugh."

"S'okay," Aspen whispered as she lay limp, her eyes closed, breathing through pursed lips. "Feels nice to have some humor. Not so much on expressing it just yet, though."

Tough as nails, my girl.

twenty-nine

IT'D BEEN two weeks since I'd been released from the hospital. The pain was bearable on most days, unless I didn't stay on top of my meds, which was usually when Cade was working. Then again, even when he wasn't around, someone usually was. My man had an issue with leaving me to the dogs, or so he would joke.

Rex had stopped by almost on the daily up until a few days ago, but I knew he was out chasing one of his skips a few states over. In the time I've been back home, I'd been introduced to Emberlyn, Shane's fiancée, and his adorable ten-year-old daughter. I swear Ember almost needed an oxygen tank the first time she laid eyes on me. She looked as if she was going to have a coronary, with how much she hyperventilated in her excitement. I'd been freaked out that she'd go into premature labor what with the swollen belly she sported. Lana Rose had been the one to get her to calm down with a zinger way beyond her years. Truly, I loved that little girl immediately. Devolin had been around more often than everyone else though. She'd brought over baby Lucas along with her a few times, and my heart about burst out of my chest when, because I hurt so bad from my broken ribs, and thus couldn't hold him, she'd laid him in the crook of my arm with his head on my shoulder, our bodies touching. I'd about cried in that moment: the sweet smell of lotion and soap mixed with baby. God, the beautiful innocence of it all.

Upon waking this morning, Molly had been acting weird, and I knew that the clock was ticking on her pregnancy and pups were imminent any day now. Even Renegade was giving her a wide berth and had chosen to hang with Cade, who was working on one of the spare rooms, as the mom-to-be was busy pacing the main floor of the house, panting on and off.

I couldn't ask for a better man than Albert Caden Summers. He'd been with me every step of the way so far, ensuring I didn't want for anything. As much as I missed the sexual intimacy we shared before that fateful day, I lived for those moments we both found ourselves in bed and discovered a new kind of intimacy—the emotional kind.

I never thought I'd find a man who would be so open with me, nor that he would accept my faults, doubts, worries, and assorted quirks. Hell, I never thought I'd be that open with anyone, but the man just made it so easy.

This morning though, I was sick of being in bed. Feeling lonely, if I were being honest, I opted to try and walk around. I felt good, and I had a hankering for a tea. Then, maybe I'd check up on what Cade was up to.

Over the last few days, I'd heard the shuffling of furniture, which must have been new as that bedroom only had a small stack of boxes the last time I'd been in it. There'd been a lot of electrical tools going off on the regular and hammering. But for the last hour or so, things had grown quiet, and that piqued my curiosity.

After doctoring myself a cup of tea, I shuffled my feet back upstairs. Pausing at my soon-to-be office door, I pressed my ear to the surface and listened in.

"What are you doing?" Cade's voice made me jump, which caused me to jar my ribs, and I sloshed scalding tea over my hands and down the front of my shirt. "Fuck! Pen, are you okay? Shit. Hold on, let me go get a cold washcloth." He ran off for the extra bathroom, mumbling other expletives and chastising himself along the way.

Returning, he took my mug from me, handed me the cloth, then put the remainder of my drink on the floor at our feet.

"Lift your arms slowly," he directed.

Next thing I knew, my shirt was well over my head and thrown to the floor and Cade was on his knees in front of me. With my less than flattering white cotton bra on display, he dabbed at the angry red marks on my stomach.

"Fuck, baby, I'm so sorry." He punctuated his remorse with kisses, his hand cupping my ass which kept me firmly in place.

My hands braced themselves on his shoulders to anchor my swirling head.

"Fucking Christ, Aspen, I can smell you," he groaned, then licked around my belly button. "You're turned on."

Because his mouth on me had me distracted, my usual sarcasm never came out. Instead of a "no shit, Sherlock," a loud mewl pushed past my lips.

"My cock misses that sweet pussy of yours, baby."

Damn I'd missed that filthy mouth of his. "We need to stop, honey," I sputtered. "I can't yet."

Cade pulled away, his eyes full of hunger. "We can't do that, but I can think of a rather enjoyable way to give my woman what she needs right now."

With no fanfare, he got to his feet, grabbed my hand, and gently tugged me toward our bedroom.

Cade

The last thing I wanted was to cause Aspen any pain, but as hungry as I was for her, I knew she was suffering just as much and there was no way I'd let her handle it herself. She'd probably jar her ribs some more. No, this was my job.

Guiding her backward until her knees met the edge of the mattress, I savored her mouth like it had been months instead of mere hours since I'd last tasted her kiss.

"Cade," she whispered against my lips before I proceeded to kiss down her front, crouching enough to be able to pull her pajama pants down and let gravity do the rest of the work.

"Well now," I smirked at the sight.

"Underwear is just another thing I need to fight with when I go to the bathroom. It's more comfortable this way, anyway," she explained, her cheeks red, her eyes looking everywhere but at me.

"Look at me, Pen," I commanded, and enjoyed the resulting reaction of her pupils dilating. "The fact that you're comfortable enough to go commando is hot. The fact that there's one less item of clothing for me to remove is fantastic. Now, sit, then lie down, baby, and let me make you feel good."

The moment she was in position, I removed my shirt, my work boots, socks, and jeans, then I carefully positioned myself between her legs, her pussy bared to me in its glistening glory.

Running my index the length of the crease of her sex,

watching the digit begin to sheen with her essence had me almost bursting my load in my underwear.

"Don't move an inch, sweetheart. I don't want you to hurt," I warned before kissing her thigh.

"Fuck, Cade, I think I could come just from you breathing on me. You could never hurt me," she urged.

Nipping her thigh, I contained her body's jolt with a smirk. "Oh, but I could make you hurt so good, baby." Before she could respond, I spread her pussy, then licked her from bottom to top, ensuring I flicked her clit before giving it a gentle suck.

"Oh, fuck!" She went entirely liquid, her hands fisting the sheets at her side.

"Don't hold back, just let it roll over you," I said before inserting two fingers inside her and latching on to her nub.

Making a come-hither motion, toying with the secret spot of hers that always made her go wild for me, it wasn't long before she gave me what I wanted—what I needed.

Dizzy with the taste of Aspen, I took my time crawling up the bed to snuggle her side, but she shocked me when her hand snuck into my briefs and circled my cock. Hooking the back of my neck with her other hand, she pulled my head to her face, close enough for her to capture my mouth, licking my lips before begging me for entry, which I gave freely.

Pulling away breathless, her eyes gleamed with so much want. "Let me take care of you, Cade."

I closed my eyes and groaned, letting my forehead meet hers. "Don't have to."

"Do you honestly think I'd leave you hanging?" she snapped, causing me to open my eyes and study hers. "I need this as much as you want it. I can't have you in my mouth—"

"Fuck me," I croaked.

"I can't take you in my pussy," she added.

"You're killing me, baby."

"But I sure can jerk you off. Don't—"

I couldn't hear any more from her, so I shut her up and thrust my hips into her hand to let her know she could have me any way she needed me. She would forever have me.

ASPEN

Heated velvet over steel.

Cade's cock throbbed in my hand, and I reveled in the small amount of power I wielded over him. It never ceased to amaze me how well we could play each other.

"Fuck, baby," he growled.

"Give it to me, honey," I whispered on his lips then took his mouth, fucking it like I wished I could fuck him properly in that moment.

Sliding my thumb over the tip of his shaft, I used the precum as added lubricant, squeezing his girth, massaging, sliding up and down to the root of him, offering a bit of a twist in my manipulation.

I swallowed every groan, growl, and moan, offering him some of my own until he spilled himself, at which point I soothed him with light kisses.

"I love you," I whispered.

Cade's eyes opened and his gaze had softened. "I swear I'll marry you one day," he whispered back, causing me to smile and give him a small peck.

Had I been left to my own devices and Cade not snuck up on me earlier, I would have been pretty quick to find out the damn man had been clever. He'd locked the bedroom door to keep me out.

Needless to say, the fact my surprise remained as such for however long it was going to take him to finish it, I ended up with much more on my plate an hour later, when Molly yelped while we were finishing up with eating a late lunch.

"Shit!" Cade muttered from the large mudroom at the back of the house where he'd set up the whelping pen. Seconds later, he ran into the kitchen where I was rinsing our plates, a large grin on his face. "Looks like today's the day, sweetheart."

A burst of excitement and trepidation took hold of me. "Really?"

"Hell yeah. She's panting more than earlier this morning, and she's now lying down as though she's going to start pushing." He walked up and wrapped me gently in his arms. "I suppose this is as good a time as any to possibly beg you to keep them all, right?"

With a harrumph, I smacked Cade's chest. "Are you insane? Seven puppies?"

He nodded. "Shane mentioned the JPD is looking to add to their K-9 unit because some of their roster are getting up in age and are due to retire in the next couple of years. I've trained for them before."

My brows furrowed. "That only takes care of two, maybe three of them, honey. What about—"

"Shane, Dalton, Rex, Bryce..." he listed. "They all said they wanted one. Granted, I'm not sure if Babyface could cut it being a doggy daddy since he can barely keep himself fed," he said about Brycen, then added, "It's why he's always gorging himself on someone else's food."

I giggled at that truth. Brycen Matthews was definitely a special character, but one whom I was endeared to as though he was my little brother. "Okay." A few more seconds rolled by, and excitement took over the small level of trepidation I'd been feeling. "It would be great to keep the babies in the family," I said. "It's sad that we'd be losing a couple of them to the force though. With the police K-9 unit taking some, I'd been hoping to keep one or two here with us, but realistically, it's just not feasible."

"We'll figure out what to do with our grandpups, but just know that we have options, sweetheart." He grabbed the back of my head and pressed his lips to the top of my head as I hugged him to me. "Right now, let's go see how she's doing." Letting me go, he latched on to my hand and gently towed me alongside him.

"Grandpups?" I snorted, looking at him from the corner of my eye.

Cade shrugged his shoulders in deference, smirking. "Come on, Grandma."

thirty

"MOM, I WANT THIS ONE," Lana Rose stated, as she gently picked up the largest of the litter that tripped over his oversized paws and onto her socked feet.

The puppies were a little over three weeks old now, and Dr. Feinstein had been off by one on his ultrasound. Aspen and I had ended up with eight pups.

"I thought you wanted the smallest one, not two minutes ago," Brycen stated from his perch against the living room wall, taking a swig of his beer.

"Yeah, but look at this little guy!" She pushed her face into his and he began to suck the tip of her nose, eliciting a giggle from the girl. "He's soooo cute!"

Aspen was on the floor with the child, surrounded by Renegade and Molly, ensuring their pups didn't get into trouble.

"The best way to pick your dog is to spend the same amount of time with all of them. They need to smell you, feel you, Lana Rose," Aspen explained. "Then, when you least expect it, your furry best friend will come to you. Probably not today, because

191

they're really not ready to leave their mother yet, but you can keep coming over to visit, and eventually, one of them will stick out." My woman cuddled the runt to her cheek, her eyes closed with an expression of bliss on her face. "The best dog is one that chooses you and not the other way around. That's what makes the best and strongest bond between a person and their pet."

Lana Rose looked to me. "Is that true?"

I leaned forward from the footstool I was currently sitting on, kissing the side of Aspen's head. "It's how it worked for Renegade and me, right, boy?"

Renegade responded with an affirmative snort, his head bobbing up as though he was nodding.

"Cool!" Lana Rose said, then placed the pup back down, picking up the next closest to her.

For the next hour, we talked about nothing much and watched Shane's daughter amuse herself by bonding with the puppies. My eyes, however, had been fused to the woman currently sitting on the floor; her back leaned against my thigh as she held a sleeping Lucas.

Aspen must have felt my eyes on her because she turned her head and looked up, a peaceful smile on her face.

"Uh, oh," Rex started.

"What?" I barked playfully.

"That look," Brycen filled in.

"What look?" I asked dumbly.

"The one like if you had it your way, I'd already be barefoot and pregnant," Aspen supplied, much to everyone's shocked gasps.

I laughed. "Sweetheart, I've been telling you once a day since you've been back from the hospital, I'm going to marry you. Is it that much of a stretch that seeing you with Lucas wouldn't make me want to make sure we have one of our own too?"

She grinned. "Not at all, but let's deal with those eight furballs first and recuperating from the latest bout of sleepless nights. Then you'll need to pop the question, followed by us getting married first," she taunted.

Smirking, my eyes never leaving her, I called out to Dalton. "Get your kid. There's something I need to show Miss Sassy Pants here before we head outside to grill dinner.

She readily handed the baby over to my friend and boss, then grabbed my outstretched hand so I could help her up to her feet.

"Before all of that though, I believe I owe you an office," I announced.

Her eyes twinkled with delight. "It's ready?"

"Been ready for an entire week now, but I wanted to wait until today so everyone could check out where my woman will be hard at work writing her future best sellers."

ASPEN

When we got upstairs, Cade took the key out of his pocket and unlocked the door.

"Close your eyes, sweetheart," he requested, then gently brushed my lips with his before taking hold of my hands. "Good girl."

I couldn't help the shiver of anticipation from the sexual undertone his praising comment had over me.

"Cade, this is completely unnecessary," I told him, nerves actually getting the better of me.

"Let me lead you," he whispered in my ear, then let go of my hands to move himself behind me, guiding me by my hips.

I could smell fresh paint, wood, cinnamon and apple. I felt what must have been an area rug of sorts under my feet, as the entire house was covered in hardwood.

Cade let go of my hips, then from much farther than I thought he'd be behind me, he said, "Open your eyes."

My jaw hit the floor at what I saw.

White shelves, so many—much more than I ever had at the cottage—lined the entire wall to my left. My collection of books, along with my own works had been placed in what looked like the order I preferred keeping them in, but they were also artfully organized and spaced out so that the occasional pottery, photo frame, or knickknack could personalize things.

Where the shelves met the far wall, a beautiful light sandy beige cuddle chair sat by the first large window, with an abundance of throw pillows in various tones of blue and aqua, and a throw in the matching hues was strewn over the armrest.

To the right of that was a small side table with a new coffee mug and a box of my favorite tea brand next to it. I shook my head at this large collection of personal touches that Cade had put into this room so far, and I hadn't even finished taking it all in yet.

As my eyes moved farther to the right, toward the second large window, I found a massive custom-built desk with all sorts of accoutrements an author could dream of, including a docking station for my laptop and a larger-than-life computer monitor. The office chair matched the accent pillows, and when I turned to face the remaining wall—the one that hosted the entrance to the room—my eyes welled up with tears.

Multiple quotes—far too many for me to count, and all from my own works—were displayed as a word collage of sorts, above another half-wall set of bookshelves, but it's what I saw displayed in the only frame sitting on the top ledge of those shelves that confirmed everything I'd been feeling with Cade had been real.

Walking up to the frame, the tips of my fingers skimmed the image behind the glass.

"These are my parents," I whispered. "Where'd you get this?"

"Had some help tracing down some of these items, but you forget I work for a security company, and we have two very gifted computer geniuses as friends," Cade stated.

Turning to finally face the man who'd done so much more for me than I could have ever asked for, I was nearly bowled over by the sight before me.

Door shut, us enclosed in this little piece of heaven he'd created for me, I found Cade on bended knee.

"Oh fuck!" My hands came up and started to fan my face in an effort to cool the burn of tears threatening to break their banks.

"Aspen River Ridge—"

My eyes went wide. "You know my whole name?"

"Just to start," he said on a smile, his eyes shining with so many emotions. "Do you want to know what else I know?"

I couldn't speak, so I simply nodded, losing the battle to hold on to my tears.

"I know that since you've nursed me back to health, I've thought of no one else but you. I know I'm happy wherever you are. I know I'm a better man because you don't hesitate to challenge me, you put me in my place, and you call me out on my bullshit. You make me smile, laugh, and fuck, but you know just what to do to turn me inside out, boiling with anger one minute, then hotter than lava to get you naked the next. My world is right only if you're in it. I know I want it all with you: the house, the dogs, the friends, and the kids. Most of all, I know I love you. I will love only you. You're it for me, sweetheart. Marry me. Marry me today, tomorrow, ten years from now. I can't be in this world without you as my wife."

"Holy shit!"

Cade's brows crinkled. "Is that a yes?"

I was a complete mess. Between tears running down my face, my mind reeling with his surprise, then his words...I ended up with the most ridiculous reaction.

I broke down into a fit of giggles before my heart finally kicked my ass in gear and I launched myself at my man who caught me, falling on his back to cushion my fall. My beautiful Caden Summers.

"Fuck yes!" I shrieked. "Yes!"

Next thing I knew, I heard cheering from outside the room's door. Grabbing my man's face, I stared into his eyes, smiling as he swiped the remnants of my tears away with the pads of his thumbs.

"Kiss me," I demanded.

He leaned up and gave me a quick peck. "Can I get my ring on your finger now?"

My mouth formed an 'O.' "Crap. Yes, of course." I sat up over his thighs to give him room to do an ab curl and sit up.

Showing me the tiny box in the palm of his hand, he pulled it open with his other, and I damn well nearly swallowed my tongue. The band was yellow gold, perfect diamonds inlayed in the band with a beautiful oval cut diamond solitaire at its center.

Cade grabbed my left hand, then lifted it to his mouth, kissing my knuckles. Next thing I knew, he was sliding the elegant piece of jewelry onto my wedding ring finger.

"It's beautiful," I choked out.

"Perfect," he added, before he slammed his mouth on mine to give me the real kiss I had asked for.

"We gonna get to grillin' those steaks any time soon?" Brycen cut into the moment.

"We want to see the ring!" Lana Rose shouted.

Cade began to laugh through our kiss and I couldn't help but join him, offering him a small peck before we pulled apart, grinning at each other like a couple of maniacs.

This was our life.

Awkward.

Crazy.

Funny as all hell.

And filled with interruptions.

But it all went a long way to make it worthwhile, that much sweeter—fulfilling. And I couldn't wait to see what this adventure brought us next.

If you enjoyed *Night Hunt*, please take a moment to let other readers know what you thought of Cade and Aspen's journey by leaving a review at your favorite retailer, or visit Goodreads.

Thank you!

* * *

about the author

Born and raised in small-town Northern Ontario, Canada, Carey Decevito is a writer of erotic romance, paranormal romance, romantic suspense, and a member of the Ottawa Romance Writers. This lover of food will throw in a bit of heat, a dash of sass, a pinch of comedy, and a dollop of real-life experience to provide her readers with a story that will mess with their emotions from start to finish.

Family and friends are her lifeblood, but Carey also enjoys conquering the outdoors, sports, traveling, and playing tourist in Canada's National Capital region. When life gets crazy, she seeks respite through her writing and submersing herself in the latest addition to her library. If all else fails, she knows there's never a dull moment with her two daughters, her goofy husband, and their cat and dog who she swears are out to get her.

She is the author of *The Broken Men Chronicles*, *Essence Extracted Trilogy* and the latest *Nightshade* series.

facebook.com/carey.writes

instagram.com/carey_decevito

x.com/ItalRT4u

goodreads.com/ItalRT4u

bookbub.com/profile/carey-decevito

amazon.com/-/e/B0092HWSDY

also by carey decevito

Nightshade Series

Night Break

Night Shift

Night Hunt

Night Hack

The Broken Men Chronicles Series

Once Written, Twice Shy

Almost Forgotten

Play Me to Infinity

To Forgive & Hold Safe

A Heart's War

Essence Extracted Trilogy

Essence Derived

Essence Redeemed

Essence Surfaced

Collections & Anthologies

Love at First Sight: a first-in-series collection